THE KILLING STRIP

THE KILLING STRIP

ANTHONY UNDERHILL

Matador
5 Weir Road
Kibworth Beauchamp
Leicester LE8 0LQ, UK
Tel: (+44) 116 255 9311 / 9312
Email: books@troubador.co.uk
Web: www.troubador.co.uk/matador

ISBN 978 1848763 302

British Library Cataloguing in Publication Data.
A catalogue record for this book is available from the British Library.

Typeset in 11pt Goudy Old Style by Troubador Publishing Ltd, Leicester, UK

Matador is an imprint of Troubador Publishing Ltd

To my mother, Jo, Gabriel, Katie, Marcus,
Kirsten, Falk and Sue.

29/10 | Schönhauser Allee

Here it comes.

'Anything,' I said.

She jerked her head to clear an obliquely cut fringe from one smudged kohl-rimmed eye. A habit she had in order to fix people fully with that unblinking stare of hers. Another U-Bahn to Alexanderplatz rattled overhead just to ratchet up the tension another notch. The sounds of the southbound metro train reached us underneath the iron girders: the whine of a 747 taxiing for takeoff and the double-barrelled report of bucking rail supports. Holding my gaze she let it pass by before she said:

'Promise you won't fall in love with me. If you do, you will die like the others.'

We were standing beneath an overpass where the U2 line breaches for air and two stops before diving again. The ivy green stanchions stood over us, angled at 45 degrees and arranged at 10-metre intervals more or less straight down the median strip on Schönhauser Allee. They looked like the wide apart legs of a dancing troop in a 1930s Hollywood musical, striking a symmetrical pose as the camera passed underneath.

Another disturbance. This time the flash of a yellow tram as it went by on the northbound side of the road with its cargo of spectral faces. The rumble of its passing went through the cobbled paving on which we stood, and where my eyes now lay, to run up our legs and shake the marrow.

It took me back to the seminal part of this story, where the journey to this point began: Warren Street tube, London. I was on the platform loitering when I should have been rushing, late for work and an apparently 'important announcement' regarding my department. Another train was coming, heralded by a gust of warm air and a localised earthquake. But I didn't move. Brain locked by a single thought. The tube train burst out into the open and soon disgorged its packed cargo – commuters spilling out onto the platform like the entrails of a gutted animal. And still I stood, buffeted by the throng with one thought still stubbornly clinging on:

To have is not to be.

And now here I was, seven weeks later, in Berlin, looking for answers, for excitement. Finding trouble.

I gave her a rueful smile.

'Too late.'

October 2 | 1989

My love,

Do you remember our last weekend together? Remember? We borrowed your Uncle's Trabbi and drove to Muggelsee. That damn two-stroke engine near gave up on us on the way! We found a perfect spot by the lake and made love, before swimming in the brackish water, and afterwards lay on a blanket to let the sun dry our naked bodies until we were discovered by those kids.

Do you remember what you said to me as we lay there under that tree? "There will be no wall between us." It burst my heart like an overripe fruit. I think about it every day. When I walk along Schwedterstrasse I imagine turning right into the bricked-up tunnel under the railway tracks. I imagine there is no barrier there, just an open tunnel, and I walk on underneath the railway line. I keep walking through to the light on the other side. And you are there, waiting for me. There in the sunshine.

03/10 | Static Voodoomatic

It was an inauspicious and unconventional start to the relationship. Then again, convention seems to be an antonym to her daily life, so where better to meet than in a toilet washroom?

In Berlin, music venues sprout up and wither all the time. As soon as a scene is discovered it disappears. Moves on before the hip crowd can harpoon it. Not only that but the venues are also notoriously shy, preferring to hide themselves away on poker-faced street fronts; more often than not failing to make their activities conspicuous, unless you knew beforehand they were there and looked for the tell-tale spume of lingering revellers.

I had found a flier in a local café for a low-key gig by a couple of different bands and had decided to check it out. The Anarchist, my new flatmate, had declined after seeing that the music on offer included post-industrial hardcore – whatever that was.

Even with a printed address the venue in Friedrichshain was difficult to find, situated in one of several old industrial buildings set back from the street. The single story building in which the concert was to be held seemed to have lost its entire ground floor and forced everyone to gather in what was once the basement. There were two entrances: one in a circular hole in the wall that led to a prefab stage, and one more conventionally through a heavy wooden door and down a plank supported by beer crates to the bar.

The first couple of sets were mired in technical problems, and I took a trip to the bathroom to relieve myself hoping things would improve.

I thought I'd mistakenly strayed into the Ladies' WC. In mitigation, not only did I have a poor grasp of German, failing even to make the distinction between *Damen* and *Herren* but also, ashamedly, was unable to distinguish between the universal symbols for the sexes – the arrow/phallus mounted circle for males and cross mounted circle for females. To further bolster the defence, your honour, may I also submit evidence 'C' – the doors themselves, strewn with various graffiti, tags and stickers obfuscating any indication of sexual orientation.

The fact that she was in there, too, didn't help.

She was neither carrying out her ablutions or utilising the grimy hand dryer. She was just standing there by the washbasin, facing the door as if expecting me, a half-cocked smile exposed in the cracked mirror, one eyebrow lifted in quizzical amusement. Those eyes alone could floor you. The rest of her features simply applied the *coup de grace*. I mumbled an apology and backed out the door. She didn't move, or say anything to oblige my genuflections. I felt as if I had strayed into a *harem*, punishable by castration and entry into the ranks of serving eunuchs, or like a Roman general standing briefly in Cleopatra's inner sanctum, looking on as she took her milk bath. I stood outside in the dark corridor not quite sure what had just happened, wondering if the whole episode had simply been the result of febrile imagining, desperately trying to cling to Polaroid snapshots of ivory skin exposed in luminescent snatches – Marc Anthony, having retreated from the Queen's ante chamber, recounting the glimpses of languid limbs in the viscous bath; legs briefly appearing out of the cream depths like a dolphin's flank exposed in the prow of a boat. Only this Polaroid was reversing its process of photographic development.

To compound my confusion I went into the 'Gents' only to discover two girls giggling over mobile phone footage who were none too pleased to see me. One barked something in German and I again beat a retreat to examine the outside of the door. It was indeed the Ladies. I had been in the right in the first instance. I went back to the original WC composing my face and a witty opening, only to discover that she had gone.

I was still mulling over the incident at the bar when the lights went out. Not a power shortage but a prelude to the next act. It was greeted with whistles from the crowd. A synthesised keyboard stopped them, soon accompanied by a simple base line and driving percussion. Then a female voice, sonorous and smoky, like Nico's for *The Velvet Underground*, filled the derelict space. A spotlight hit the makeshift stage and the band's singer. Her. She crooned into the mic, gripping the stand the way a drunk clings to a lamppost. Those eyes, lost, seeing nothing – the thousand yard stare of a Vietnam veteran. The small crowd stood rapt, some bobbed their heads in accompaniment to the rhythm, as in deference to the incantations of a High Priestess. A few more appreciative whistles followed as they recognised the track. The band were playing a Joy Division number, *Atmosphere*. I leaned up against the bar and sipped my beer, never once taking my eyes off her. A Thom Yorke solo number followed. *Black Swan*. She sang 'This is fucked up' with a small trace of an accent that was hard to place, but with little trace of emotion. Then they effortlessly segued into the haunting opening verse of Echo and the Bunnymen's *Killing Moon*, and those watching lapped it up.

As they went through their repertoire of lounge lizard takes on alternative noir tracks she very rarely strayed from the microphone, only once to drink something from a plastic cup, and she never addressed the audience between songs. They didn't seem to mind, the aloofness of the *chanteuse* only enhancing her hold over them.

And then it was over.

As if a spell was broken sudden sound burst out from the audience – whoops and cheers and claps followed by animated conversation as the crowd drifted over to the bar. The band, still on the stage, put away their instruments unhurriedly, unhooking cords and carrying amps, instantly forgotten. She, however, was gone.

October 3 | 1989

My love,

I can often hear sounds coming from the other side. Car sounds, for one. The engines on the west side sound different. They sound powerful, not so distressed. Not like they are going to give up on you at any second. At one section I sometimes hear music. Western pop music. English words. So close! I imagine you there, on the western side, dancing to it, opening the windows for me to hear. Like a moth to a flame I am drawn to it. I see myself scaling the backland wall, then the signal fence, and heading towards the music; across the column track I go, past the tank traps, past the watchtower, across the last bit of wasteland to finally reach the border wall. It would take only half a minute to make the crossing at this point. But I soon snap out of it, as we can't linger long in one spot. If we don't make our cross-over point at a certain time our colonel writes a report. Such sweet music, though. So full of life. No doubt singing of love.

06/10 | Find Rusty Regan

'Remember me? Doghouse Reilly, the man who grew too tall.'

The Anarchist and I were sitting on our kitchen table chairs – cheap plastic fold-up jobs. Only we weren't sitting in our kitchen. We were sitting in a disused mortuary.

'Remember?'

We weren't the only ones there, either. Over forty others were arranged on a motley collection of brought seats, including stools, deckchairs and cushions. We were all sitting facing one way, faces lit in flickering spectral light. Silent, attentive, eyes fixed on the bare wall on which the black and white film was projected.

'Let's go in. I've got a key. Swell, huh?'

We were attending a 'secret cinema' night, a concept perfect for Berlin with its innumerable opportunities for innovative screening venues. The Anarchist was on the coveted mailing list and once a week was notified, on the day, of the film to be screened and the one-off venue it was to be screened at. BYO chairs and popcorn.

I loved the film but I'd seen it before and my attention couldn't help wander about the space we were in – sporadically and solely lit by the old school projector the organisers had brought – examining the grid of refrigerator holds to our right, some with their dusty doors eerily ajar. My attention then fell on the crowd, hip and young, for whom the morgue was remote and alien enough a place to allow themselves a frisson of speculative wonder. Some were even sitting at the back watching the film on a rusty gurney.

My eyes then gravitated toward the front of the audience where one outline had a trace of familiarity. A woman's long straight black mane. A man to her left, who almost matched her in hair length, turned to her and whispered something. She said something back, face serious. A brief profile was caught in celluloid backwash. Her.

'That's her, the one I was telling you about. Near the front,' I whispered to the Anarchist. 'The singer.'

'You going to talk to her?'

'If I get the chance.'

When the film ended people took their seats and made their way with torches out into the night, picking a route across the fractured floor to the exit. We walked over broken tiles and brick dust, gingerly stepping over the odd hypodermic needle. It was hard to make her out in the absence of the projector's light; we hadn't brought any illumination and had to meekly follow beams on floors directed by others.

I'd thought I'd lost her until the crowd had re-congregated on the platform of the nearest metro station. She was by herself, going the other way to us, but the station's LED display indicated I had a few minutes until ours arrived so I made my way over to her. She was clutching a purple suede cushion to herself to ward off the cold, looking down the track. I decided not to say anything in my faltering German.

'I seem to keep bumping into you in unusual places.'

She appraised me warily, no sign of register, so I followed up with: 'I liked your Joy Division cover the other night, but I think "She's lost control" would have been more appropriate.'

It was a flippant remark, the first thing that popped into my head. I was unaware then of its prescience.

A trace of a smile. 'I'm not in control. I don't pick the songs,' she said.

Eager to fill in the gaps I said quickly: 'Who is ever fully in control?'

In the metro station's light I got to take her all in for the first time. Even though she had a curvesome figure that turned other heads on the platform it was the face that could have graced the silver screen. Oval, symmetrical, with an unobtrusive nose, generous lips and, of course, those eyes. I thought she could have been of Turkish extraction as there is a large Turkish community in Berlin, or perhaps Persian. I felt there was something quite quixotic, though, about wanting to get to know her – even then – but something inexorable about it, too.

'You ever thought about playing in the UK? You would be popular there.'

'Maybe one day. We're just starting out.'

'I couldn't tell. The band were pretty tight.'

It could have looked slightly odd, a man with a fold-up chair chatting to a woman with a cushion on a subway station. But we were surrounded by several other people carrying seats of various kinds. Some were even using them while waiting for their train to come.

'I'll write down where we are going to play next,' she said, one arm reaching into a coat pocket.

'Thanks,' I said, not really meaning it. I had taken us down the sycophantic fan route, and was wandering how to pull out of that cul-de-sac into private number street when her movie companion turned up with a white leather pouffe and two train ticket stubs. It was the bass player from the band. He eyed me with barely concealed hostility, giving me the once over. I did the same, noting the tall, thickset figure, black leather trench coat, faded *Clockwork Orange* t-shirt and t-bone sideburns.

'You smoke?' he asked with a non-German accent.

'Not if I can help it.'

'English?'

I nodded an affirmative, thinking of something to say to her instead.

'He was at the gig,' she offered, writing on a small piece of paper, writing arm clamping the cushion against her side.

'What are you doing in Berlin?' the man asked.

'I ask myself the same question.'

'And... come up with any answers?'

'Looking for inspiration, I suppose.'

The man dropped his pouffe and pulled his hair back into a pony tail, a scrunchy between his teeth, as if preparing for something serious. There were elements to his demeanour that made me want to brain him with the folded chair, but such thoughts were soon banished by the Anarchist calling out to me. My train had come first. Time to beat another retreat.

'My ride. Nice to have met you. Again.'

Her chaperone ignored me, wrapping the scrunchy around his bunched hair, looking up at the station's display to see when theirs was due. She offered the scrap of paper and an amused smile at the testosterone stand-off. 'You too. I hope you find your inspiration.'

The train was busy and there was standing room only. Not for us, of course. Sitting on the kitchen chair barrelling through the bowels of Berlin I studied the carefully folded piece of paper she had given me. I realised I hadn't even asked what her name was. It was on the paper, though, along with her mobile phone number.

October 06 | 1989

My love,

I have been put on duty on a watchtower near Wollankstrasse. It is sweet torment for I can see over the strip to the border wall and the lights at night on the other side. Why, when you look at lights in the distance, do they twinkle like stars? I think of you as one of those stars. I think of you standing in a window on the other side, looking out at the lights on our side of the wall and thinking of me. It is seven months and thirteen days since you were smuggled out. I would risk everything for one word. Just one scrap of paper with your handwriting on it. The other side is so close there. Sometimes I get this urge to leave my post and run, run, run! Across the wasteland, the last remaining part of the strip, and vault the second wall with one single leap. But I know I would not get far. My fellow guardsman would not hesitate. And there is no car with a secret compartment waiting to take me over the Bormholmer Bridge. I cannot make the same contacts. Impossible. They pay most attention to those on guard duty. Especially me. Especially now.

10/10 | Tobacco trance

She took me to a shisha bar in the district of Wedding. I could not see much as we entered as a heavy pall of smoke suffused its space, along with a sweet aroma. Turkish and Arabic eyes from cloud-clogged booths surveyed us as we went past to take our seats. The bar's owner was beside us in seconds to take our order. She did the ordering.

A hookah was brought and placed on the low table between us – a three feet high water pipe that consisted of a tubular glass jar at its base, connected with a rubber seal to an ornate metal stem, on which rested a small circular tray and ceramic dish. Attached to the stem half way up was five foot of hose with a wooden handle and silver mouthpiece. On the other side was what looked like a valve. She uncoiled the hose from the pipe and took a long, languid draw. I looked at the hookah's summit. Charcoal coals sat on the top of the clay dish packed tight with unseen tobacco leaves. The coals glowed as she inhaled. Tin foil was wrapped over the top of the brown dish shaped like an upturned egg cup, the foil punctured by numerous tiny holes through which the smoke from the glowing coals was drawn. The coloured water that filled two thirds of the vase now bubbled, adding to the feeling you were witnessing an experiment by a deranged scientist. Soon smoke filled the top third of the vase like the froth of a continental beer. Finally she exhaled, blowing a nimbus up toward the uneven stucco ceiling crafted, it seemed, to imitate the interior of a cave, before handing the pipe to me. I was about to put it between my lips when she said:

'Do you want to swap the smoking tip?'

She indicated a plastic nozzle in a cellophane wrapper on the table, identical to the one already slipped over the metal mouthpiece. One each.

'Should I need to?' I asked.

A wry smile came in response. I put the pipe in my mouth and inhaled, my gaze focusing on the metal stem of the hookah. It was moulded to taper and bulb in sections leading up to the tray – all concentric rings and curves like stacked pagodas, some inverted, from a Buddhist temple. I looked at the jar bubbling away. The water was obviously there to cool the smoke, which left a pleasant fruity taste in the mouth.

She read my face. 'It's apple flavour.'

I breathed out. 'I like it.'

I took another drag to prove it. She watched me imbibe with those eyes punching through the smoke. Those goddamn eyes.

A silver tea urn arrived and two glasses of peppermint tea were poured out for us from an ostentatious height. It was meant to help aerate it, apparently, thus enhancing the flavour.

As I smoked I listened to the Middle-Eastern ululations coming through the bar's sound system, and thought I caught snippet of something that sounded familiar.

'Eid? Is he singing about Ramadan?'

'The song? No, no! He's singing about his love. Maybe you mistook "Habibi," – that's Arabic for beloved. *Eid* is where the man can't eat or drinking anything,' she said. 'The Qur'an dictates they must fast on the last day of Ramadan.'

I imagined her in a veil. Those eyes cried out for a frame. 'And the women?'

'Stay out their way. You ever deprived yourself of something?'

'Not through choice.'

'That's the problem in the West. Too much choice. Not enough self control. Deprivation feeds the soul, it nourishes the spirit. Makes you think about things a bit more, makes you appreciate things. Something you like tastes even better when you deprive yourself of it. Imagine a cool glass of water in the desert. Everything is better when you moderate it. Food, drink – even sex.'

'That particular fast is not a self-imposed one,' I said hastily.

The coals glowed as she inhaled. Her eyes seemed to do the same. Inscrutable eyes that hovered in the blue-tinted smoke. She passed the hose, smiling at me. In the subdued lighting of the café I didn't know where the pupil ended and the brown iris began, making her orbs ink wells that made me stir in discomfort on the cushions and draw heavily on the pipe, hogging it for longer than was polite. One perfectly tapered black eyebrow went from acute accent to circumflex. The aquiline nose crinkled in accompaniment. I stifled a cough and handed the hose back.

She worked the plastic part over the mouthpiece along her lips. The bulbous tip resembled a nipple, taught with cold or arousal. She tweaked it with her teeth before slipping fleshy lips over it to take another lungful. The lips then pursed to form an oval before blowing a few rings out toward me.

'I can see you've done this before,' I said.

'It's as part of Arabic culture as the pint is to you English.'

Covert glances through the haze were being sent her way. Sporadic glimpses of the Middle-Eastern girl sharing a shisha with the white guy who couldn't smoke. Questions were asked, speculative answers given, and met with soliciting nods and wisecracks. If she heard them she didn't let on. Whispers in the court of Cleopatra.

'What brought you to Berlin?' I asked her.

'Several things. A change. In a strange city you start afresh, be a new person if you want to. In a city that doesn't know you, you have no baggage.'

'Why would you want to be someone different?'

'Haven't you ever wanted that? To start afresh. Be someone new? Isn't that why you are here?'

'Yes, I suppose so.'

'I like this song. So beautiful,' she said, drawing my attention back to the music. She hummed along for a while.

'Who is it?'

'This is Abdel Halim Hafiz. Famous Egyptian singer. It's a song about a lost love. He's singing… "And something in the night makes me lose myself…" His story was a sad one. His family wouldn't let him marry his sweetheart when he was younger. And when they were allowed, before they could wed, she fell sick and died.'

I changed tack with her. 'You told me you used to perform, back in Beirut.'

'Yes.'

'Did you sing songs like this?'

'Similar. Sometimes.'

'Did you have any fans?'

She blinked. One the rare occasions when she did. Long lashes augmented by kohl briefly shuttered the eyes to form a starburst in double negative.

'Some. I must go to the ladies,' she said, suddenly slipping out of the booth.

'Make sure it is the ladies this time,' I said.

While she was gone the owner came over to change the coals and I took another lungful, this time the smoke feeling a little harsh. It was probably only a minute but she seemed to be gone for quite a while. Where the hell was she? Had she

17

gone, grown tired of her English cat's paw? Boots on stone floor announced her return. Steady even steps. The sound of heels: one of the best sounds known to man. It seems to touch something in the limbic part of the brain, conjuring up in the mind arched stockinged feet, taut black leather and a zipper that ran up the side of a tensed calf. Men's eyes tracked her progress back to our booth.

She sat down and said immediately:

'I have to tell you something.'

Here it comes.

'One of the reasons I came to Berlin was because of my singing career in Beirut. I used to perform in the nightclubs in the Muslim district near the old Green Line-'

'The Green Line?'

'That doesn't matter. It's just that Beirut was split, just like Berlin used to be, with an invisible wall. Used to be called the 'Green line'. Muslims on one side and Christians on the other. I sang in bars on the Muslim side, but I'm from a Druze family. I had fans, was working on an album. Then...' She trailed off.

'Then?'

'An admirer started sending things to me. He'd be in the front row on most shows. Always requesting to see me afterwards. I tried to keep a distance, but he... he is an important man. He was insistent.'

'He got too close to comfort?'

'You could say that. It was best I left.'

'Do you miss Beirut?'

'Of course. It's my home.'

'Will you go back?'

Her eyes glazed. 'Eventually.'

I wanted to know more, ask more. But the STOP signs were suddenly flashing. Instead I offered a weak crumb of solace.

'He'll forget you. Get infatuated with someone else.'

'Maybe.'

She was not with me then, I could see that. She was somewhere else, in an apple-scented tobacco trance. I smiled at her and sipped my tea, wanting to feel myself being drawn up with her into the shisha fog bank.

01/09 | More news from nowhere

The sensation started slowly at first, then grew to become a suffocating, all-consuming fugue. The words and the people around me began to distort then fade as I felt myself dissipate, like the misty breath on a cold day. I floated up from my chair, and for a while drifted in the unseen eddies of the conference room, meandering with the motes of dust caught in the light of the overhead projector. Then up to the ceiling I rose; up, up and through the air-conditioning duct to pass along the arteries of the building, past the humming cables and toxic insulation. Indistinct, formless, free…

A knock on the door of the conference room pulled me back to my seat. The door partially opened and a man's head poked through and nodded in my direction.

'Sorry to interrupt, but there's a call for you. It's urgent.'

My colleagues' eyes followed me as I made my way woodenly around the conference table to the door; some, it seemed, with a hint of envy, even though the news might be bad.

Could not be worse than this.

Redundancy in the form of a Powerpoint presentation outlining necessary downsizing and the virtual dismantling of our entire department.

The eyes spoke to me. The eyes said:

'Anything. Anything rather than this.'

I looked back at them wanting to say aloud the words that

had been rattling around my head all morning, ever since they had come to me on the tube platform:

To have is not to be.

Not that that would have offered any comfort.

'Who is it?' I asked my colleague as I slipped out of the meeting room. Closing the door he gave me a curt look.

'I didn't ask.'

'Why not, you useless cretin? It's an urgent call, possible emergency, and I am in the process of being fired, along with most of my bloody team!'

I didn't say this. I said 'Okay,' and sent tomahawks spinning off to lodge into his disappearing back.

On my desk there were three post-it notes stuck on the phone's handset. A terse scrawl informing me that my girlfriend had called. Again. A light was winking at me indicating a call was waiting. I punched it. 'Hello?'

'Burgundy or beige?'

'I'm sorry?'

'Burgundy or beige?'

'Nel?'

The voice dropped an octave in impatience. 'Burgundy or beige rug for the living room?'

'I don't... Look, I'm in the middle of an important meeting. You said it was urgent.'

'It is. The offer ends today and I took time out from work to get this.'

'Whatever you prefer.'

'Don't be blasé.'

'Burgundy.'

'I think beige. Will go well with the ottoman, don't you think?'

'Don't go overboard. We're just renting the place.'

'There's an option to buy. I spoke to the landlady the other day and we'd get preference.'

'Let's not get hasty, now. We've only been there three weeks.'

'What are you trying to say?'

'I'm saying let's not rush into things.'

'Don't be like that. Nothing wrong with planning ahead, babe. Oh, and I meant to tell you that Sam and Martha are coming over tonight.'

'Tonight?'

'Hope you don't mind. And Sam, her new *beau,* is with the other agency, remember? You said you weren't happy where you are. It might be good to network. Contacts. Besides, it gives Martha and I a chance to chat about the wedding. She's having trouble finding an affordable florist. Oh, and Steven and Holly, too.'

We are like stars, slowly drifting apart.

I wanted to say this to her. Instead I said, 'You mean Lord and Lady Haw-Haw?'

'No, that isn't the one. I said mustard. Two by three!'

'What?'

'Oh, I was talking to the assistant here. Utter nincompoop. Doesn't know her *Aarnio* from her *Elica.*'

'What time?'

'I said any time after eight. A small soiree. Informal. We'll do *hors d'eourves.* That reminds me, can you swing by Tesco on your way back and get that nice Spanish red? What was it that we had at my mother's? With the fancy label? Camino del Mar, wasn't it? Oh, and can you possibly look for some endives from the deli if they have any left?'

This is all rhetorical. I look down at my desk. Instead of jotting a shopping list on a post-it I have absently drawn a figure suspended in a noose, as if playing a game of hangman in reverse.

'I might be late. Got a lot on here.'

'I'm sure you can get away. You're not *that* important, are you? See you at seven, babe. Kiss.'

The line went dead.

October 1st | 1989

My love,

To think I used to be a true believer in the Socialist cause. It shames me to write that I was.

The Russian Empire is crumbling. Other Soviet states are breaking off. Gorbachov is relenting. But our leaders stand resolute. Our glorious leaders. Pah! Just give me a clean shot. Just one chance. Erich Mielke is visiting the Stadium of the Youth of the World to watch BFC Dynamo play this Saturday. I imagine climbing one of the floodlights and picking him off among the other dignitaries. But I must keep calm for you, my love. I must not do or say anything seditious to attract the attention of the Ministry for State Security. Ever since you left I catch suspicious glances from fellow guardsmen. Only Matze treats me the same. But then he is a drunk and he knows I know it.

When I talk on the phone I am always careful. In-between gaps in conversations with your family I listen for the tell-tale clicks of someone else on the line. Informers are everywhere. There is even one in our building. Remember Anke, the one who complained when we had a party? Works at the dairy. Her! Tobias told me and I trust him. She meets a young man in the park on Tuesdays. Certainly not a lover.

Remember that nice artist on the second floor? He's gone. Just left one day and never came back. Some people cleared *out his apartment yesterday. Everything. Anke didn't like him, always telling you about the company he keeps. Remember? Now he's gone. Bitch. But I don't think she's the only one in our street betraying their neighbours. Even now. I would like to shoot them all.*

When this state falls, there will be a reckoning. But I must remain calm. Must not draw attention to myself. I will not do anything to jeopardise our coming together. It will be soon, my love. I am sure of it.

14/09 | Offensive posting removed

Thank you, Tim Berners-Lee. Now we are all interconnected. Now we know what's front page news in Cape Town. Now we can shop and collect 'friends' like shiny buttons without even needing to venture outside. Now we know what the surf's like at Banzai, the meanest surf break on the North Shore of Oahu (we can see it, streaming live from a webcam – just about). Now we can read poorly researched, speculative, inaccurate, unbalanced information and assume it to be the gospel truth. Now we can register our stupidity and expose our spleen to the world in pitiable bile-flecked postings beneath unrelated news articles or uploaded video clips. Now we can pick a city we have never been to, but always wanted to experience, and search for private advertisements for apartments in those far-flung places.

Here's the advertisement I found in a random search on the Berlin section of a popular networking site:

Short-term rent in nice apartment. Share with antichrist.

At least that's what the roving eye scanned for me. Then on second glance I saw that it was in fact *anarchist*, not antichrist, which didn't seem much of an improvement. Why on earth would anyone advertise that? I wondered. Well, it got my attention. At least he was up front about his beliefs. It would come out of the wash at some stage, I supposed. Perhaps anarchistic tendencies would become evident when a discussion started over who's turn it was to do the washing up.

That's what the net needs, mind. More honesty.

Desperate male, 39, NSOH, seeks equally desperate female for last throw of romantic dice. Attached picture taken in favourable lighting five years ago by eight-year old son.

And

This mail is not actually from a girl or a friend and the product advertised therein will not make your penis bigger and, if you are cretinous enough to buy it, will in fact give you a nasty rash that will eventually force you to go and see a doctor, and to whom (who will be female, BTW) you will have to explain just how you got it.

I decided to email the guy, just for the hell of it. I received an articulate and sane response, plus attached pictures of the apartment, which looked spacious and relatively neat.

I called him. He spoke perfect English and seemed disappointed that I was not from Scotland. But he was willing to consider me as a flatmate, nonetheless, especially if I could make the rent and deposit up front.

Berlin beckoned.

02/10 | Lost weekend

FLIGHT EZY2107 BERLIN STAY IN LOUNGE

Flight. It was flight all right.

I can see myself staring at a rather sorry looking egg McMuffin sitting in its wrapper on the table in front of me, and thinking: *How appropriate.*

That it barely resembled the munificent specimen depicted in back-lit glory above the counter summed up modern life quite succinctly. My example seemed to have all the requisite elements, though: battery farmed egg and ersatz cheese slice the colour of a Nagasaki sunset, plus muffin. But the muffin looked as though it had been only exposed to a mere rumour of heat and then accidentally sat on by an overweight member of staff before being carelessly wrapped and deposited onto my tray. That it was missing the advertised dimensions and failing even the lowered criteria of fast-food edibility, sitting there soggy, limp, dejected, also seemed appropriate. It summed up my state of mind perfectly.

Lingering doubt was gnawing at the intestines, filtering up through the body like an acid burp.

What the hell am I doing?

As I am sitting there in a hard-backed plastic chair under fierce strip lighting – all designed to get you to eat up and shove off *tout suite* – I'm ruminating on what I am about to leave behind. A nascent career in London; a slowly nurtured and burgeoning bank account – now the seemingly never-ending student debts had been paid off; a step on the rung of the property ladder; an ambitious down-payment on a saloon car with five litre engine, catalytic converter, leather upholstery and Bluetooth connectivity; a slowly nurtured relationship with promise of safe coupledom; a growing circle of friends and an increasing level of respect and note from peers and family alike. 'So what does your son do for a living? And are there plans for children?' etc.

All tossed away on a whim.

Flight.

The point of travel for most is, understandably, all about the destination. Get there and get there fast. And yet, part of the pleasure of transit is just that: being in-transit. It's that sense of existential limbo, of being temporarily unencumbered by what has transpired and what has yet to transpire; a spatial and temporal vacuum where the weight of the world is temporarily lifted. You are neither at A nor B, but somewhere in-between.

And yet we are all too anxious to get to B, ignoring the opportunity just to soak up that sense of being unburdened by the past or the future (perhaps it is the way, in modern flight, for example, we are processed at airports and packed tightly in planes that takes the edge off of our ability to appreciate travel). But for a few hours up in the lower reaches of the stratosphere we are allied only to a sense of expectation and anticipation of what B offered. And among many things, B offered renewal, re-invention, re-birth.

'Kane's gonna get fucking caned!'

I looked over at a table nearby and noted something of Blighty I definitely would not miss. Say goodbye to the English gentleman and shout 'oi!' to the English lout, permanently altering the perception of us abroad; thanks to, among other factors, cost-cutting education 'reforms' and low-cost flights. The easyjetset. This lot were off on a stag weekend in Amsterdam.

'What, like spanked?'

There was general mirth at – let's call him Darwin – Darwin's observance of the pun. Other heads around the McDonald's restaurant turned in their direction. Frowns from couples, parents, heads shaking in disapproval at the loud, expletive-laden prognosis of the group's upcoming stag weekend. I noticed only one who seemed to be registering the opprobrium from surrounding tables. Maybe it was because he had not drunk as much. The others were too inebriated and too entrenched in the collective security of the pack to notice – or care.

'Keep it down, guys.'

'Don't be so gay, Lyle.'

'Yeah lighten up, Lyle. We're on fucking holiday!'

'You should see your outfit, Kane. Ha ha!'

'I don't want to look like a tit.'

Too late.

'A giant tit; now *that* would be funny.'

'Where would you be able to rent a giant tit?'

'You'd find something like that in Amsterdam, no worries.'

'Why are you worried about how you look? Not like you gonna pull this weekend.'

'He wants a last shag, don't he? Before he gets hitched.'

'There'll be time for that. Besides, the hookers don't care what you look like, as long as you got the dough. Even Lyle will get laid.'

'I'm not fucking a whore,' one stag said, semi-earnest.

'I bet you will, Kane. Jeoff told me they're some real stunners in the Red Light District. Been twice. Behind glass doors, they are. Right on the street.'

'You'll be too stoned to get it up, Mike.'

'Skunk, man. Like, super strong.'

'I can take it.'

'Yeah, right.'

'I wonder if we'll get time to see the Anne Frank Museum,' the one called Lyle said, and instantly regretted it. The chatter stopped. The pack stared. Someone threw a French Fry, ketchup coated on one tip like a matchstick. It struck him on one cheek leaving a thin smear. Much mirth at this.

'Shut up, Lyle.'

'Anne Frank!'

'Muppet!'

'Anne Summers, more like.'

'Sex shops there make Anne Summers look like fucking Help The Aged, man. Gimp outfits, dildos shaped like fists. I've seen documentaries.'

'I bet you have.'

'You've seen the pornos more like.'

'I bet he's into that – gimps and fist fucking.'

'Perv.'

'Fuck off.'

'Come on, show us the outfit.'

'Not yet. Not yet.'

'Make him wear it for the flight.'

'No way!'

'They won't let him on.'

'Ahahaha!'

'Go on, gis a peek.'

'I'll show you one part of it.'

Darwin reached out from under the table and pulled up from a bag the head of a sex doll: a shock of blonde curls, the eyes wide in surprise, the mouth an unsubtle crimson 'o', reminding me of Munch's *Scream*.

A Spanish couple newly arrived at a table not far from theirs stared open-mouthed. Their son, four, maybe six, had stopped playing with his newly acquired plastic giveaway out of his Happy Meal to also watch. A miniature Ronald McDonald suspended in grimy fingers among empty cartons, napkins and spent ketchup packets.

'Fucking ace, Jase.'

'I'm not fucking carrying her around. No way.'

'Let me get a pic. Bigger tits than your wife, Kane.'

'Go on. Blow 'er up!'

'You wait till you see his outfit. Classic.'

They sauntered off to the nearby bar for more beers, raucous shouts whip cracking off the low ceiling and glass fronts of clothing stores. The more sober one, Lyle, looked back to see an African gentlemen in a flawlessly ironed staff shirt clearing up the detritus of their meal.

It was 10 a.m.

Enjoy your trip, boys.

I looked back down at my forlorn muffin and thought of divergent paths. Like them I could just disappear for a weekend of excess, put it down to a mental aberration on return. Come back with a sore head and list of ribald anecdotes. Would boost the water cooler 'cool factor' no end. Add an element of edginess and dynamism to my Facebook profile. Then I remembered the emails, the phone messages before my departure for the airport, the sit down heart-to-heart with an incredulous girlfriend and I heard the sound of flames licking at the beams of bridges.

Divergent paths. I imagined our boozed up emissaries of In-ger-land appalling all who they came into contact with on their two-day sojourn, staggering along cobbled streets, tossing empty kebab wrappers into the canals and pointing at semi-naked girls exposed in red-strip neon booths, egging each other on. Should they be allowed to travel abroad if they don't meet a basic criteria of respectability? Is this what freedom of movement is about? The ability to piss in someone else's fountain? I imagined Britain's Nanny State tipping into totalitarianism and revoking passports for such protozoa. Not only that, but revoking their right to pass on their DNA. Neutered. Chemically castrated after failing basic intelligence and social skill tests. But a grim smile is quickly wiped when I thought of where I was flying to, and the quasi-Nietzschean eugenics of a past regime. I quickly banished the thought and considered taking a bite out of my muffin to soak up the rising bile.

2nd October | 1945

I have not been allowed outside for two weeks now, and there is so much I miss. The sun, of course; the wind in my hair when I ride my bike; my friend Lotti; birds singing in trees; playing catch with Mika, our Schnauzer, in the park; my mother and father.

Grandpa says it is not safe to go outside because of the Soviet troops, so I have to stay in the roof attic of our building, which is cold and smells of old mouldy things and has spiders and mice. I do not see the mice but I can hear them running about, nibbling on things they should not nibble on. I am not scared of them, and often I talk to them and try to reassure them and coax them out of their hiding places. But they will not pop out and say hello, even though they take the cheese I leave out for them in the night, which is sometimes all I have to eat. Sometimes I do get scared when the candles flutter and throw shapes on the roof from the wooden beams and the things left up here. Mother's mannequin sometimes looks alive in the corner of my eye in the candlelight. I have dressed her up from some old clothes I found in a box, so it is alright when I catch her moving. I imagine she is having a peek, left and right, over the boxes to see if I am alright, before returning to her slumber.

Soldiers were in our apartment building again, today. I heard them talking in their strange language, things breaking, my grandpa protesting and telling them to leave. Grandpa told me they are looking for precious things to steal and for girls to make their girlfriends, and that is why I must hide. Most of the soldiers are much older than me, although grandpa says they would not mind this. But I would.

03/10 | Pramlauer Berg

Here's what the property types would make of my new home:

'Exceptionally bright and spacious two bedroom apartment. Inexpensive relative to London or New York, it is located in a desirable area close to all major amenities. Retains charming period features with high stucco ceilings and stripped floorboards. Close to sites of historical interest, including one of the last of the Nazi bunkers to fall in the Battle of Berlin in WWII, which you can see from the apartment's balcony. Also, a surviving remnant of the former Wall separating Soviet East from Allied West Berlin is a mere hundred metres way.'

What the property types would omit to tell you:

'Neglected front denotes what to expect from the building's interior. The lock for the building's entrance does not work and can be opened with a well-placed application of boot. The Communist-era plumbing may contain residue of lead and will protest with a solemn racket whenever you or one of your neighbours decide to impose on it with a turn of a tap. Be warned: there is a tendency for water supply to be rescinded when too many residents turn taps at the same time, so shower experiences my fluctuate in heat and intensity. Further, the building is next to a waste recycling depot, home to over twenty garbage trucks that head out at 6 a.m. six days a week past the building, giving the impression of a Panzer brigade on manoeuvres. Above you is a fat obstreperous woman who stomps around her apartment (the obvious downside to wooden floorboards) and is mother to an incredulously fawn-like 16-year-old daughter who flirts on the stairway with every male who happens to pass. Below is a jovial Estonian who is happy to disclose he is a part-time Internet spammer (assuming the identity of Russian women looking for love) and proud father off three boisterous children. Next door to you is a Pole who rarely ventures outside. He is called 'Spiderman' by the other tenants. So named because one time he tried to scale the outside of the apartment to get into an open window of his apartment on the second floor when he thought he had locked himself out. He only succeeded in kicking in a window on the ground floor trying to clamber up a drain pipe and scare the life out of the young couple living there. After much discussion he was offered a place to sleep for the night with the couple, only to discover that the keys to his apartment were in one of his pockets all along. He'd been drunk then and, we've been reliably informed, has been drunk virtually every day since, evidently trying to banish the memory of a wife lost in a car accident ten years ago.

Did we mention you would have to share the apartment with a Scotophile Anarchist?'

As the Anarchist and I made our way to the local café I started to take in my new surroundings. The deep gorges of connected streets; the ranks of imposing apartment buildings with their starling nests of balconies; the peeling facades, some with neglected facia and scrollwork; the uneven flagstones ready to trip a leaden-footed pedestrian; the burst crust of macadam exposing the roots of street side trees. Most omnipresent of all were the tags by graffiti artists marking their territory. Some showed talent, brightening the space, decorating the ground floor walls and still shuttered windows of dull tenement buildings. Some were just spastic scrawls; angry teens with no voice in society. Many were in English.

THATZ

HERO

SHY GUY

Some recurring icons: the raised fist; the flaming roller-skate. Some sprayed in improbable spots indicating tenacity and inventiveness – over the lip of pedestrian bridges spanning railway lines, up scaffolding to deface newly painted walls. In all its many forms, graffiti was almost everywhere in Prenzlauer Berg.

PASST AUF YUPPIES!

I noticed a few Tibetan flags about, too. Reduced to tatty rags by years of neglect.

We were finishing the tail-end of a lively debate as we walked. I found it refreshing. I could not remember the last time I had had such an impassioned discussion about anything.

'Only a thin membrane separates us from barbarism, even now,' I said. 'Between moral imperatives and the wilfulness of the beast, between orderly society and anarchy-'

'Hey, don't say anarchy. You mean chaos. Anarchy isn't chaos, mate, it's small scale co-operation. There's socialist anarchism and individual anarchism, there's-'

'So you keep telling me. But to be honest, anarchism seems to be the right idea for the wrong age. We haven't evolved far enough yet to co-exist harmoniously without the steering hand of government. Things are still too precarious.'

'That's your opinion, friend. But it's already worked as a social model in other countries. In parts of Catalonia, for example, before Franco... mind the dog shit!'

On entering the café we were greeted by African music. The

37

interior was well lit by tall, bare windows which exposed several aspects: an unadorned dark concrete floor; pockmarked ascetic walls the colour of unused mustard, the colour changing four feet up, like a water mark left by the retreating tide; a motley collection of fifties furniture; a scattering of square tables, some formica topped, around which were clusters of utilitarian dining chairs, an even split of faux leather reds and greys; a wooden panelled bar shaped like a sawn-off hockey stick; low-hanging lights suspended over the bar; a forgotten section of wallpaper surviving in the corner; a crescent of suspended faded purple drapes protecting the patrons from the encroaching cold air from every entrance or exit. Very considerate, very continental. What wasn't considerate was the steady, insistent *tap tap* of laptop users on other tables. Bluish faces lost in a half-baked thesis or the Next Great Novel. In an open plan office this sound is lost in the general white noise of white collar life, but in a café with muted music and low conversation the sound was like the gnawing of rats behind wainscoting. It reminded me of mobiles with mp3 players on London buses. Progress seems to be marked by technology's ability to come up with more and more ways to either disconnect people from direct interaction with other human beings or blight public spaces with sonic pollution.

'Wankers,' the Anarchist said to his black coffee, absently scratching an unruly beard. His unkempt thatch of head hair, equally bushy, added to the overall impression of a pallid face peeking through a grizzly fizz of undergrowth.

'I thought you said you liked this place.'

'I did, but it's changed. You used to get punks in here. Proper punks. It was a political place. Left-wing. Organising demos, that kind of stuff. The police stormed this place once. We had to climb out a back window. Now…'

A loose button on his jacket shook as he twisted in his chair to survey the café. The thread swung briefly like the stalk of an eye socket.

'It looks like a pretty chilled place,' I said. 'Lots of artist types and students.'

'Artists.' He spat the word out like a melon seed.

As if to illustrate his point on the café's decline the purple drapes parted and a Trojan horse appeared to lay waste to Bohemia. It came in the shape of a four-wheeled black nylon and chrome bugaboo. The pram, the size of a SMART car, wheeled in with a woman in her thirties behind it wearing a macramé'd cap and talking on a mobile. The entrance elicited no stir of alarm from the other café dwellers, no rush to arms or even just dismayed looks. Invasion and subsumption was met with casual indifference.

The Anarchist turned in his seat and grimaced. You could read the resignation on his face. This café, the last bastion, the last redoubt against the Prenzlauer Berg Pram had been breached.

Prams – 'The Yuppie scourge,' as the Anarchist called them – are everywhere in this Berg. Must be something in the water. A disproportionate number of mothers parading around the streets. Prams, given self-appointed right of way, often side by side, bullying their way along the main drag, forcing other pedestrians to the sides, ploughing through flea markets, double parked with trolleys in supermarket isles. Mewling whelps and stentorian mothers, wearing that medal of baby bile on one lapel and a dark ring-eyed look of entitlement: Biological clock beaten. Genetic imperative met. Evidence to the Anarchist of Yuppie takeover and the Berg's precipitous gentrification.

Mother ordered a latte and scattered feeding bottle supplements on a table nearby, while still attached to the phone. The newborn – small, pink and mercifully asleep – was cradled on her lap.

'Another yuppie mouth to feed on the planet's teat,' said the Anarchist.

'Your hangover's worse than I thought.'

'There used to be riots outside on the street. Barricades. Police gate crashing May Day celebrations. We fought for these streets. For what? Now look at it. Look who's taken over.'

I play Devil's Advocate. 'It's called progress. Happens in every city. Inevitable. It happened to Greenwich Village in Manhattan; it happened to Primrose Hill in London. It will happen here. Move on. The squatters and the artists and the students will.'

'You weren't here in the early 90s, my friend. If you were you would be sad to witness the difference; at what the area has become. Someone has to take a stand.'

Listen to him. The indignant rancour of a socio-political scrooge. But I know the root cause. I had no right to be indignant myself, to feel his militant opprobrium, but I felt some of it nonetheless. Maybe it's what it represents, what is being lost. A part of me rails at it, too, because for me every pram, every three-wheeled baby Humvee I had to dodge on the streets was a reminder of my own patent failure, my occlusion from that comforting circle of social norms. I gave up the game of musical chairs while others found their seats. Children, mortgages, jobs – all indexes of adulthood and achievement. All rejected.

'So you want to come to this gig?' I asked him, fishing a flyer out my pocket.

He screwed up his face at the set list. 'No. Not my type of music.'

'I think I'll check it out.'

'Go ahead.'

The mother laughed at something the voice on the phone said and sipped her froth-topped coffee. The pink thing squirmed and yawned. I looked away and tried to affect the air of an indifferent local, noticing instead the Anarchist's shoulders were tensed, as if he was anticipating that first scream filling the café's space.

At least it would drown out the sound of tapping keys, I thought.

October 3rd | 1989

My love,

I saw a woman on Greifenhagenerstrasse today. She was wearing your dress. I followed her for a while. I could not help it. From the back it looked like you. I imagined you'd been caught and sent back. My heart leapt at the possibility! Is that wrong of me? As I got close, though, it was clear it was not you. Not as beautiful. But I still followed for a while, enjoying watching the sway of the hem of your dress, listening to the sound of heels on the pavement. I wanted to walk along side, just walk, and escort her to wherever she was going. It reminded me of walking with you to redeem your food stamps on Monday mornings, of the smell of freshly applied home-made scent and the conversations about incidental things. It was a quiet street so the woman must have heard me. She looked behind her at me and suddenly looked frightened. She hurried on, picking up pace, her head down. My uniform! I wanted to shout out to her, tell her it was alright, but I couldn't. I crossed the road and turned into a side street, feeling ashamed.

I wanted to relive those moments. That's all I wanted to do.

10/10 | Fi Youm, Fi Shahr, Fi Sana

I was still feeling a little dizzy from the shisha, but it was a nice feeling. We walked aimlessly, talking, our breath misting in the cooling early evening air, as if our lungs had yet to expel all the hookah smoke. The Berlin streets were set out for us in solid, straight-backed rows. Solemn trenches with four floors of sporadically lit windows on either side. Curtains seemed rarely drawn in Berlin, revealing glimpses of hanging bulbs and passing heads. Some windows had balconies, often crammed with pots. Mortified plants left to fend for themselves in the meagre space, fighting off the bitter cold, waiting to stretch out and receive the light when it briefly crested the tops of adjacent buildings.

Glowing tips of spent cigarettes fell to the street like a half-hearted ticker tape parade as we passed underneath, skirting dog faeces and bikes locked to railings.

Her long legs did a half step followed by a hop to avoid a brown smear. 'So much shit. Why don't they clean it up?'

'Come on, I'll give you a piggy back.'

'A piggy back? What's that?'

I bent over with my back arched to her.

'Jump on my back and I'll show you. Come, your Highness, your mount awaits.'

'You're crazy.'

'No crazier than you are.'

'Gentleman,' she mouthed to me with a smile.

She jumped on and wrapped her arms around my neck, laughing. I found my balance and carried her down the street. A few strands of jet black hair fell down to brush the right side of my face. A faint trace of a scent reached my nostrils.

'You said you were a dancer as well as a singer in Beirut.'

'Uh huh.'

'What kind of dance? A belly dance?' I half-joked.

'Close,' she said, her mouth close to my right ear. 'It's called *Raqs Sharqi*. Maybe I'll dance for you sometime.'

I straightened my back to let her slip to the ground. 'What about now?'

'Here?'

'The street's clean here.'

'I need the music, the costume.'

'Improvise.'

Calling my bluff she performed an impromptu shimmy right there on the street corner. Humming softly, looking at me, arms raised, wrists gyrating, hips jutting.

'It's all in the waist,' she said. 'Need a butt to do it, not like those sticks you see on the western catwalks. Only a real woman can dance. It's all about what you don't show. It's more more sensual, more suggestive. The hands are important, too.'

I tried to imagine her in a wisp of chiffon on a smoky stage in Beirut. But instead my mind drifted offstage to a figure sitting in the front row. Watching intently is her admirer. Sipping a Turkish coffee, he nods obligingly to obsequious hosts, his yellow eyes never leaving the stage and the dancing girl with the beguiling voice.

'I'd like the proper dance sometime,' I said to her.

'We'll see,' she said tossing her head. Behind her the bare tree tops were back lit by the last embers of the day, like capillaries in a bloodshot eye.

Lost weekend | Lyle

Café Monument was enjoying the torpor of a late Sunday morning in Amsterdam. The bustle and business of Saturday's market day on the -*straat* was long forgotten, replaced today with a half-empty languid calm, which Lyle was about to augment with a dose of sensimilia, once he had finished rolling his fat but rather tatty looking joint.

He loved this café, far from the touristic throng, tucked away in the slim folds of the Jordaan. Full of narrow streets and artist's studios, the Jordaan had the bucolic charm of a former working-class area that had not been overly gentrified, and the café was the Jordaan in microcosm. Best of all, even though it was not a dope-dealing café, the bar tender and patrons did not seem to mind him smoking weed there. At least, not on one of its tables outside.

He lit his conical object-d'art and let his slightly bluer smoke meld with the tobacco smoke of the regulars. Bliss. The café dwellers, playing backgammon, reading *de Volkskraant*, the Dutch national, over a cup of strong black coffee or just smoking, gave Lyle an indulgent look and carried on with their respective concerns. Even the resident cat seemed to be in a good mood. It was curled up on the window sill, drinking in the sun that occasionally brushed through the thronging clouds to stream down and pick out the rising tendrils of Lyle's joint. The ginger tabby stretched and yawned, recovering from nocturnal exertions, no doubt. *Just like me*, Lyle thought. He inhaled deeply then blew a column of smoke at the cat. It loved it, he was sure, getting gently stoned in the rectangular sun-trap. What a life; free of cares.

Lyle had measured out his Amsterdam weekend so far in coffee spoons and Rizla paper and was enjoying it immensely. The same thing could not be said for Kane, the groom. It had been a catalogue of disasters so far. Jason, the 'Best Man', had only booked two rooms at the hotel, which was full, so there'd been a dispute, soon after arriving from London, on who got the beds. Then Shane, who had declared he'd 'travel the world in one night' by having sex with women of all colours and creeds, had got so stoned in the first coffee shop they'd been to he'd fallen off his hire bike and was now testing the limits of his medical insurance policy at a Dutch hospital. Then, that night, outside the Banana Club, Jason had gone for a piss and had disappeared. And there was still no word. Without the dubious organising abilities of the 'Best Man', Saturday had degenerated into a dope and alcohol fuelled bitching session, and Lyle had walked away to leave the remaining stags to it.

He put them out of his thoughts and instead considered the pleasant time he'd spent by himself this weekend. It made such a welcome change. Coffee spoons. How many days had he measured out his life in coffee spoons and post-it notes at his god-forsaken desk at work? Or in train ticket stubs and abandoned newspapers – the detritus of commuter life? How many weekends had he wasted, for that matter? He realised his life was nothing but a succession of lost weekends, of torpor, recovering from alcoholic excess; routines without purpose: pornography; computer games; shopping trips with testy girlfriends; reality TV and football analysis shows. All without meaning. All gone. He would not be able to count them and he did not want to. Instead he rested his joint in the crook of an ashtray and went inside to order another coffee.

The new bar tender, a welcome change to the earlier saturnine tender who had given him unwelcome looks, was a middle-aged man with greying shoulder-length hair and a crooked smile. He seemed to love all things Yankee-doodle, with his cowboy belt buckle and Neil Young CD collection. He had a stack of them behind the counter now and was playing 'Harvest Moon'. *Good choice*, Lyle thought – the album fit the morning's mood perfectly.

How to do justice to a Brown bar if you have never seen one? The Dutch have a word for it, Lyle learnt: *gezellig*, or 'cosy'. It's all about creating an ambience that relaxes you, makes you feel like you have stepped into someone's living room. And this, it seemed, could only be achieved over decades. Everything had a lived-in feel, all the edges smoothed like a Torquay pebble he once found for his girlfriend, shaped like a cartoon heart. It all felt effortless because it was. Brown bars are not like the many London pubs he would normally frequent – interior designed facsimiles of hipsterism – they were more organic. And the key to achieve this *gezellig* feeling, it seemed, was principally through lighting. No 80 watt bulbs in these establishments; instead soft lighting from honey-coloured bulbs, diffused through smoked glass shades, were used. Candles figured prominently, too; molten sticks placed all over, allowed to deliquesce and reform like magma from a benign volcano. And the more melted wax on surfaces, the better the bar. Older = better. What's more, *gezellig* didn't just apply to the inanimate. The bar staff also lived by the code. No rushing around keeping the patrons imbibed. They'll do it at their own pace in their own time – and that was fine with the patrons.

Lyle could imagine staying here indefinitely to let what he had left back home gradually discombobulate and knew he would feel little remorse. Perhaps it was the inoculating effects of dope, but he imagined it all with complete apathy: His girlfriend's anxious bewilderment, the office speculation, his friends' consternation.

Back outside he took a sip of his coffee to offset the dryness in his throat. It was not sweet enough, so he poured another stream of sugar from the dispenser into his cup, watching a circular section of foam on top of his *koffie verkeers* sink and dissolve under the weight of the accumulated crystals. A *koffie verkeers,* he had been told by the bartender, was a 'wrong coffee'. Lyle had ordered a coffee (they all spoke embarrassingly good English in Amsterdam he had soon discovered) and was asked whether he wanted milk with it. A splash of cow juice made it instantly 'wrong' in many Dutch eyes – perhaps for negating its potency. The Dutch liked their coffee as strong as the Italians, and Lyle was thankful for that; one narcotic helpfully counteracted the soporific effects of the other.

He took another toke and luxuriated in the sounds of guttural Dutch around him. To be surrounded by conversations he could not understand was comforting to him as, even if it was loud, it was not distracting as he could not understand its nature. It allowed him to get lost in his thoughts.

Finding solace as an alien, an outsider, Lyle felt exotic; yet he also felt a kinship with those around him as he watched the patrons talk through the haze of his, and their, smoke. As one sense is deprived, so another is amplified, becomes more keener, more attuned, and Lyle started to be aware of other ways to decode the conversations around him, in non-verbal signs – the second, supplementary language. Smiles, gestures, postures – what is said in what is not actually said. And overall, to him the non-verbal signs coalesced into one message: a big thumbs up for Sunday from Café Monument. Everything was going to be alright.

A few spits of rain came down and, as Lyle had finished most of his joint, he decided to retreat inside. He found a table in a corner and eased into a chair. Slowly sinking in a happy haze, Lyle let his gaze wander about the compact bar that had become his home for the last few hours, and let details of the bar sink in: the layers of A3-sized posters for theatre productions and gigs gummed on top of each other to form a vertically glued tome of advertising history on some sections of the café's walls. Cut into them and you could count Amsterdam's social rings. On to the collection of crushed old beer cans growing rust in a bird-less bird cage tacked to the wall above his head. On to a wolfhound curled about its cowboy booted owner standing at the bar, the dog never taking its rheumy eyes off the insouciant cat now also inside. The cowboy boot (its wearer, perhaps a friend of the barman) rested its silver tapered toe top on the brass foot rail, a ring-choked hand gripped the bar's hand rail, another lifted a *biertje* (a beer, one third full of suds, as was the Dutch way) to heavy whiskered lips. Up to a framed black and white photograph in one corner behind the bar Lyle's gaze went. Winston Churchill looked down indignantly at him, sans cigar – hence the ire – his face babyish, his stare patriarchal and accusatory. Quickly on to, equally curious, a morning star hanging by its chain next to Winston's frame; below that car stickers from the States – 'Zappa for President' and 'Don't mess with Texas' – ran long the spirit carrying and dust encrusted shelves. Another frame at the other end: a sepia tinged beatific smile of an Indian deity. A garland curled about the frame, its flowers withered from the rigours of time and incessant smoke.

The term 'Brown Bar' derived from the fact that the walls

and ceilings were coated by what looked like a brown lacquer. This was merely the result of years and years of smoke from patrons and the innumerable candles that had coated the place, a caliginous compliment to the predominance of dark wood furniture. Part of a brown bar's charm was its undeniable history and resistance to change. In the U.K. you'd only find pubs of equivalence tucked away in the farthest corners of the British countryside, unreachable to the more malign tentacles of modernity, the 'refurbishments' that blight city drinking establishments with their indentikit gastro pubs or faux 'Oirish' charm.

Lyle looked back up at the picture of the Hindu god and was reminded of another face in a more ornate frame. He had happened upon it whilst wandering the cavernous Rijksmuseum. It was of a 16th century courtesan, and it had captivated him. The painter had given her a thin spread of teeth and an angular poise with her torso slightly forward. Her head was lifted somewhat to better splay the ample front, the low U of her top garment complimenting a knowing look. The non-verbal message of the picture said to him: 'Concentrate on me. Look closer.' The grin was fixed, unequivocally wanton – extremely provocative, no doubt, for the time.

Lyle was drawn from his reverie by an increasingly uncomfortable erection. He shifted in his seat to alleviate the discomfort and hide the swelling. *Dope doesn't normally do this*, he thought. *What's this all about?* He hadn't had sex for a week now or, now he thought about it, masturbated either. That was it: Sara hadn't let him in, piqued at his last minute notice of plans to go away on the stag weekend. He hadn't done it for a whole week. Then Lyle remembered where he was; that in this city there was a place for men with urges.

His mobile rang. A polyphonic ring tone that drew

everyone's attention. He spent a while locating it from one of the many pockets in his jacket before answering.

'Kane?'

'Where the fuck are you?'

'I'm in a café.'

'Duh. Where?'

'In the Jordaan.'

'Where the fuck's that?'

'Near the centre. Where are you?'

'I'm next to the canal.'

'There's millions of them.'

'*The* canal. The street where the Bulldog is, smartarse.'

'Oh, the red-light district.'

'Near.'

'No, that's the red-light district.'

'Well I am not *in* the red-light district, Lyle. I don't see no red fucking lights.'

'Alright, alright. Keep your hair on. What's left of it.'

'Shut up. You heard from Jason?'

'No. You mean he still hasn't surfaced? Bloody hell!'

'Yeah. I'm starting to freak out. And it ain't the dope.'

'Shit.'

'Stop poncing about in other cafés and get your arse over here and join me and Mike for a smoke in the Bulldog. We gotta decide if we contact the authorities or not.'

'Alright, I'm coming. I've got some stash already.'

'So bring it.'

'How's Shane, by the way?'

'I'll tell you when I see you. This call will be fucking expensive.'

Lyle finished his coffee and waited for the swelling to subside slightly before leaving. When it did, he got up to pay for his coffee. The patrons followed his departure with level gazes.

17/10 | We don't negotiate with the state

I gave it the customary couple of days before calling her again. No answer, so I left it. But I couldn't stop thinking about her. She didn't call. I tried again some days later. A woman's voice talked to me in German but it didn't sound like hers, so I passed my mobile phone over to the Anarchist.

'It says the number is not recognised. Please try again.'

I checked the dialled number. It was the one I'd been given and the one I had already spoken to her on.

'Maybe it's switched off,' I said hopefully.

'You wouldn't get a message like that if it was.'

It was a low. It didn't help that I had called her from a mausoleum either.

On the way to Kreuzberg, the Anarchist and I had stopped off at Treptower Park where there was an impressive Soviet memorial to fallen comrades. At one end two futuristic looking marble-clad portals stood, with statues of kneeling soldiers at either base. They flanked wide steps down to a broad stretch of paving with five squares of green, edged with topiary, the effect from the top of the steps seemed to be to imitate legions of perfectly arranged troops. Lining either side were sarcophagi with reliefs depicting acts of Communist heroism and sacrifice. At the far end stood the grandiose focal point, a forty feet high bronze statue of a Soviet soldier set up on a circular stone mound. Up a flight of steps and directly underneath the statue was a small mausoleum where flowers and wreaths collected.

We looked up. The soldier, sans helmet, had a broadsword in one hand and a child cradled in the other. At his feet was the first equilateral cross I'd seen in Berlin, or rather the smashed remnants of one. I was instantly reminded of my flight over from the UK. My tired eyes had briefly gone lazy and the patterns on the fabric on the passenger seat in front had merged and rearranged themselves for me. A discernable new pattern had appeared. Orange right angles on slate-grey, merging, touching to reconfigure into an unnerving reminder of the darker elements of my destination's history. My subconscious had somehow ominously reconfigured the pieces for me to form a swastika, subliminally registered in a headrest on an easyjet flight to Berlin. I'd tried to appease my unease by reminding myself that the symbol had originally had a more benign import. The swastika that adorned Hindu or Buddhist temples, for example. But then I wasn't flying to New Delhi, was I?

'You like her, eh? You shag her?' the Anarchist said as I stuffed my mobile into a jacket pocket.

'We only had one date.'

'So?'

I didn't reply so he said, 'Ah, you'll meet another chick. German girls like English guys. Even unemployed ones.'

'I can make next month's rent, if that's what you are thinking of.'

'No I wasn't. But you haven't really told me what you are planning to do over here.'

'Learn German. Write a book.'

'What about?'

'I don't know yet. A novel.'

'Pah! No-one reads novels anymore. Navel gazing for the intelligentsia, while real life passes them by.'

'Thanks for the vote of confidence.'

'Well, how can I say something positive if you don't know what you are going to write about yet?'

'I'm working on it.'

'All so-called artists just want to get laid. Showing off to impress the girls. Why do you think some cavemen painted pictures of mammoths on cave walls?'

'To brighten up the space? Cro-magnon interior decorating?'

'Because they weren't as good as the others at killing mammoths, at providing for the womenfolk. They just wanted to get laid as well.'

'Well I'm not going to impress her with my mammoths. I haven't started anything yet. And besides, I liked her because she was, is, different. She's… stimulating. We all need someone to share life's vicissitudes with.'

'Viciwhat? You just want to get laid! Don't dress it up in bullshit.'

'And you don't want to?'

'I don't want any trouble. Women are too much bother.'

'She's quite a woman.'

'She's trouble.'

'How do you know? You haven't met her.'

'I saw her and you've told me about her. Trouble, Englishman.'

I looked up again.

'It's an impressive statue.'

'Yeah. But the hypocrisy makes me want to puke.'

'Without the Soviets to take on the Nazis-' I started.

The Anarchist cut in. 'They weren't liberators. They were looters and rapists. The Wehrmacht did a lot of bad things in the Caucuses and the Soviet forces let their troops exact revenge across Prussia. Over 100,000 women were raped in

Berlin alone. Young, old, pregnant – even Nuns. It didn't matter. A whole city laid to waste in retribution with the women taking the brunt of the abuse; while the other Allied nations sat back and did nothing.'

I looked across the memorial.

'And now it's all forgotten. Now all that's left are a few plaques.'

'And thousands of sixty-year-old Berliners with unknown fathers, don't forget.'

It was an unsavoury thought and the Anarchist, obviously thinking the same, quickly touched on another subject. 'I really want to see Stirling one day.'

'Stirling?'

'Stirling, Scotland.'

'What made you think of that?'

'Because there's a memorial to William Wallace there.'

I know he's a Scotophile and can't help bait him. 'You mean the statue to Mel Gibson?'

'What?'

'The statue there is of Mel Gibson. You know it was based on the movie, don't you? They have a statue of Mel bloody Gibson as testament to Scotch heroism.'

'It's a monument to the leader of the Scotch resistance to English butchery. You hung, drew and quartered him in London, you bastards. Burned his guts in front of him while he still lived. I went to the place where you did it. It's a meat market now.'

'I wonder how they managed to preserve the meat for so long.'

'How many Bravehearts did you execute across the globe, Englishman? Where didn't you piss off and persecute the indigenous peoples?'

'I don't celebrate the fact that England, Britain, turned two thirds of the globe pink. I'm not going to apologise for the indiscretions of previous generations, though, and neither do I expect you to.'

But he wasn't listening, and instead lustily burst into a proud rendition of the Scots' national anthem.

'Send them homeward ta think again!'

Around the base of the statue two young Russian couples frolicked and took photographs perched on each other's shoulders, the girls screaming as the boys took in turns in a struggle to keep their heavy frames upright for a photograph.

Two guys arguing about an actor and two couples balancing on bronze laurel wreaths at a memorial to sacrifice: the irreverence of youth.

17th October | 1945

Memories and dreams are like butterflies. They flutter about and are often elusive, but when you catch them they are beautiful to look at. Butterflies come to me here in the attic sometimes and I am happiest when they do. Sometimes they are just little, like how grandma used to hide little chocolates around the living room for me to find. Under a cushion, behind a curtain, nestling in the decanter set, in-between the magazines or inside the tall clock where you had to be careful not to stop the swinging pendulum with your hand. I would find them all! That butterfly makes me feel really hungry. Another baby butterfly. The sounds in the living room. The tick tock of the tall clock; the crackling sound of burning wood in our fireplace; an afternoon play on the radio. Those sounds always made me feel cosy and sleepy.

Other butterflies are not so welcome, and I hastily let them go. Most of those are about my mother.

17/10 | Kollektiv! Offensiv! Subversiv!

On to Kreuzberg, another 'Berg' with a strong alternative past: communes, street parties, police no-go zones and May Day riots. The area still had an edginess to it, but that slow tsunami of scaffolding was rolling over the area, with its accompanying flotsam of cement mixers, skips, palettes of masonry bricks, lintels, RSGs, drills, mastic guns, wall brushes, dust sheets, tile grouters, polyfillers and emulsion brushes. Building by building, street by street. There were pockets of resistance – a commune turned cooperative housing project here, a mural covered façade there – but the futility of it was disheartening to my tour guide. Just like Prenzlauer Berg, the money men were moving in and the magic was moving out. I walked with a disconsolate Anarchist as we revisited old haunts. The place he had stayed in was gone, or at least was now a refurbished apartment building with no trace of its previous non-paying tenants. He took solace from the odd black and red anarchist banner he spotted hanging limply from several apartment balconies, and from a squat around the corner that was still holding on, its boarded up windows covered with graffiti and flyers for upcoming concerts to be held in its basement.

'That used to be my favourite bar,' he said, walking up to a glass fronted boutique for children's clothing. 'They held punk concerts there on a small stage in the corner.' He pointed to a spot where a waist-high rack of assorted mini dungarees and brightly coloured romper suits stood, then turned his baleful stare out onto the street.

'You wouldn't get a Mercedes or a BMW parked here in the early nineties. They would have been destroyed a second after they'd parked. Now look at it.'

The street certainly had its share of upmarket cars, but overall it looked a pleasant, tidy, well-appointed street. Nothing overly salubrious or ostentatious, just smart and clean. The front of most buildings proudly displayed new licks of paint, like a teenager experimenting with makeup for the first time. There were a few remaining buildings with their original brown stone or dappled concrete fronts, but they were in the minority. A whole street of the same must have looked quite depressing. I told him as much.

'But it wasn't what was on the outside that was important, it was what went on inside,' he said before dredging up an oyster of phlegm to adorn the front of a BMW coupé for emphasis.

'All burnt,' he muttered.

'But there's still trouble here, right, on May Day?'
He shook his head. 'It used to mean something, but now it's just an excuse to get pissed and smash things up. There's no politics behind it. Just riot-tourists from other parts of Germany; pseudo Anarchos and Turkish kids looking for a rumble.'

'Well, at least there aren't as many prams around here,' I said.

A few streets on he threw an arm in front of me shouting: 'Stop! Halt!' I looked around expecting to see a rapidly approaching bike or tram, but all was quiet.

'What is it? What's the matter?'

'Look down.'

I looked down. Set into the tarmac was a line of cobbled stones. The line ran past us on either side. To our left it bisected the street, to our right it went on for twenty metres before mounting a pavement and curving around the corner at the junction to another road.

'The Wall?'

'The Wall.'

'Twenty years ago we would have had to have stopped here,' I said.

The Anarchist shook his head. 'Twenty years ago you wouldn't have reached this far. You would have been shot crossing the death strip to reach this wall. We are on the GDR side.'

I looked at the cobbled stones. 'And this is all that is left.'

There are some remnants of the Wall left in Berlin, but for all of its 155-kilometre length a scant few metres are all that remain. It seems the authorities were desperate to eradicate most evidence of the city's shameful separation, and reluctantly left the odd segment for the tourists to gawp at. Like Hitler's bunker (now a car park without a plaque), it is history that some Berliners would rather leave behind, while others were already starting to lament the eager dismantlement.

I tried to imagine living where a wall bisected your street, your 'kiez', your whole city; where you literally could not go from one side of town to the other. I imagined a partitioned London; a wall running from Barnet down into Camden, Regent's Park mushroomed with watchtowers, splitting Oxford Street and Soho; over the Thames and across through Lambeth it would go, separating families and lovers. Picadilly Circus sealed off, the advertising hoardings used instead to display the valour and industriousness of the East Side to the less fortunate and exploited citizens of the West. And if you lived on the West Side and you wanted to leave the city to go to, say, Brighton, you had to apply for a pass as your entire half was encircled by wall. I found it hard to countenance.

Some would say such an occurrence in history would have been unconscionable. I'm not so sure. Brits who declare proudly that Vichy France and its collaborators would never have happened to Blighty obviously don't know what happened in Jersey.

That brought me obliquely to New York. I saw a concrete curtain falling across Manhattan, the Borough divided along 79th Street, partitioning Central Park; across the East River it went, down the other side, following Newtown Creek before running the length of Metropolitan Avenue, then cutting South to JFK. You take Brooklyn and Staten Island; we'll have Queens and the Bronx – and we'll exchange agents on the Williamsburg Bridge.

If there is such a thing as the Metaverse, where alternate realities are played out in other dimensions as real as ours, then there is one world where a young man is standing on the point of a former partition trying to imagine what it would have been like if Berlin had been carved up instead of New York, and wondering how the citizens would have dealt with it. And he is shaking his head, thinking: 'Never. It would never have happened in my country,' as he takes a broad step across the symbolic line of demarcation on 79th and Broadway.

October 17 | 1989

My love,

Today I patrolled the strip along Bernauerstrasse with Matze. Nothing remains of the dynamited church your mother went to. As I drove he offered me something in his flask that was not water. It smelt of Schnapps. I declined and we drove along the strip in silence for most of the time. I was angry at him, especially when he waved to some of the watchtowers we passed with a stupid grin on his face! If we had been stopped and he was discovered to be drunk he would have been sent to military prison and they would have thrown away the key. I would be disciplined, too, for not turning him in for rehabilitation. Eventually he said to me something like, "They try to swim across, try to fly over with hot air balloons, they have even dug tunnels underneath to get across. All from our side. Have you noticed no-one ever tries to break into our side!" Drunk fool. Did you meet him at the May Day party? I continued to ignore him for as long as I could but he still persisted with his observations. I finally snapped. "They don't need to, do they? They could just apply for a pass and stroll across the checkpoint. No western guard would stop them."

He wouldn't shut up. "If you saw someone running across the strip now, what would you do?" "From the west or the east side?" "Either." "I would shout out a warning to them. Tell them to halt immediately." "And if they didn't stop?" And do you know, I'd never really thought about it. It is my job. My *job! And I had not really thought about such a thing happening. Had you? It has happened often. Even this year in March, just before you left. Remember? The news travelled up the strip quickly. Traitor terminated whilst penetrating border defences. Terminated. We never talked about it. Perhaps it was too painful for you to mention. Of course I got the GKM directives with regard to border violations. But I had not really thought about such a moment actually happening. "Could you shoot an unarmed citizen in the back?" Matze kept badgering me with this. Could I? Could I? "If they didn't stop when I called out to them," I said. Matze laughed and pointed his rifle out along the column track and shouted out, "We don't have to shout a warning. We are told to shoot on site. Even women and children, because they could be human shields. I'd shoot their kneecaps off and watch them crawl to the Wall. I'd let them try to climb it with their smashed legs and then I'd finish them!" He laughed at his own joke and nearly fell sideways out of our patrol vehicle. I wanted to swerve off the column track and into a tank trap. I wanted to see that look wiped off his face.*

19/10 | How long is now?

Evidence of personality is on almost every Berlin street. My favourite is the thought and time someone gave to blacking out the edges of several red cycle lights to turn them into the glowing shapes of hearts. And like the graffiti, flyers are everywhere in Prenzlauer Berg, too. Flyposters for upcoming concerts or resident DJs, self-made stickers with website addresses, free rooms to let taped around traffic lights with tearaway strips like protruding teeth; group meetings, obscure movements, singers, artists, Buddhist teachers, the obligatory lost pet, badges denoting football or political allegiance, notices for aikido self-defence courses, yoga classes, imminent protests – on lampposts, bollards, traffic lights, telephone exchange boxes, parking signs, litter bins and building site plasterboards. Slapped on, slapped over then stripped away by the elements or rival fly poster boys to layer the streets with a peeling bark of semi-legible information.

Once I had seen the Anarchist notice and rip down an A4 poster for an obscure right-wing group popular in the Brandenburg area, but mostly the ubiquity of the flyers made them disappear into the fabric of the street. There was one poster, however, I could not ignore. It stopped me dead in my tracks when I saw it. I stared at the picture for a while as if daring it not to be who I thought it was.

Initially I thought it was a MISSING poster. A black and

white photograph dominated, heavily saturated with contrast, with simple typography below. I got closer. It was a head shot: long bare neck, big loops of half-braided hair, a messy crown of a garland and calm, candid eyes looking out at me. It was her all right. It was a notice for an art gathering in the Tacheles, a renowned ex-squat in Mitte. I went straight there.

Her picture was there, she wasn't. And neither was the photographer who took it. She was pride of place in a small gallery space on the fourth floor. Most of the other photographs were moody shots of disused buildings or silhouettes in tunnels. Hers was the only portrait shot and as such she leapt out at you the second you walked in. No one was there, so I asked around in the adjoining rooms that were mostly being used as active studios for artists cluttered with easels and canvas boards and the unwanted detritus from a few installations in the making. No one seemed to know who the photographer was. I wandered about the floor trying to ignore the odour climbing up the stairwell – the rising damp of a piss-stained basement. The walls were obliterated by graffiti and posters, the floors covered with the sodden confetti of discarded flyers.

I tried a couple of unlocked doors at the other end of the corridor. One opened door revealed another space for artists, this one full of oil paintings of headless torsos in varying states of undress. A thin wail blared through an opened window from the artistic welder's coven outside; a single operatic voice going up and down the scale, accompanied by a modern discordant score. The sort of music (at that decibel level) you'd expect to hear when you broke into a serial killer's hideaway out in some God forsaken wilderness.

A disembodied voice said something in German, so I used my stock response to German in reply:

'Entschuldigung, ich spreche kein Deutsch.'

'You like my boobs?'

I hadn't noticed the man sitting behind one of the larger canvases. He had a gnomic posture, a high forehead with a retreating tide of sandy hair and the look of a cabin fever sufferer. He gestured with the headless torso of a Barbie doll toward a triptych of breasts each with blue aureole.

'Yes, they are very nice,' I said.

'Where you from?'

'England.'

'Ahh.' He nodded approvingly, as if this confirmed my ability to judge the aesthetic qualities of a mammary gland.

'You?' I asked.

'Lithuania.'

'Ahh.' Ahh yes. The home of the perfect pendulous breast.

'You want my boobs?'

'Well…'

'I saw you looking at them. You have a good eye. They are my best boobs.'

'They are very good. Very… likeable.'

'How much do you think they are?'

'I'm sorry?'

'My boobs. How much?'

'How much is that painting?'

'Yes.'

'I don't know. I'm asking you.'

'Name your price. The value is in the eye of the beholder.'

'I am not really looking for artwork for my walls. And to be honest, I do prefer a bit of context when it comes to nudity. You know, what's around the breast as well as the breast itself.'

The grip tightened on Barbie. 'I see.'

'I am more into photography.'

Knuckles around Barbie whitened. 'I see.' He looked at me intently for a while. 'There is work by a photographer on the other side,' he eventually said.

'I know. There's no-one there, though. Do you know the photographer?'

'I know him to recognise him, but I don't know him to say "I *know* him."'

'I see.'

'You can ask downstairs. They will know.'

The woman's wailing from outside was reaching a crescendo. I wasn't exactly enjoying maintaining eye contact with the artist but I equally didn't want my gaze to rest on another breast, so I looked at the headless Barbie in his hand instead and backed out slowly.

'No boobs?'

'No boobs today.'

'How about a donation?'

He pointed to a spot directly behind me with Barbie's torso. I turned and saw a mug with a few coins inside on a table by the door. The words: SAME SHIT DIFFERENT DAY were emblazoned on the glazed ceramic.

'Whatever you think,' the man said.

'The value is in the eye of the beholder, right?' I said.

'Right.'

I put in ten euro cents and left.

Lost Weekend | Lyle

The wind in his face cleared Lyle's head somewhat. He picked up pace on his rented bike, the quintessentially Dutch and ubiquitous black one-speed 'Granny' bike, and made his way out of the Jordaan and onto one of the city's canals. He could cut straight across town to get to the Red Light District, but had found navigating by the semi-concentric canals a surer and more pleasant way to get around. Bouncing on the cobbled streets, he took the outer canal for a while before cutting in to the innermost canal that skirted the city centre proper and would take him almost all the way round to his destination. Four main canals semi-circled the city like a series of misshapen horseshoes, on or around which Amsterdam's older beauty resided. Lyle remembered the names of them and which one to take by thinking of the derivation of their Dutch names in a sequence from the inside out: for him the *Singel, Heren, Keijzers* and *Prinsen Gracht* were the 'Single man', the 'Kaiser' and the 'Prince' canal. It was the 'Single man' that would take him round to the Red Light District.

Crossing a small bridge Lyle gave his sizable bell a few tweaks to disturb some dawdling tourists and a few curious pigeons and felt like a local. Tourists were everywhere: heads bobbing out of maps to gaze up at cornices like Meercats, meandering in couplets over bridges, lingering in the middle of the road to alternately take pictures. Blighting the backdrop of the curving, tapering canals with cagoule-clad grins. You.

Now me. Now you again. Just one more. The locals didn't see them, gliding past on their bikes with not even a glance, let alone a tinkle. It seemed the use of the bell was an admission of weakness for them. The tourists weren't noticed the same way they didn't notice the clusters of pigeons following the crumbs left by stoned Brits with the munchies, clutching a burger or a packet of chips coated in mayonnaise.

She was looking up at a street sign, at the juncture of two narrow roads and Lyle saw her late. He veered off with a screech of protesting brake blocks onto the pavement, narrowly missing a bollard.

'Oh my God! I'm so sorry.'

She pulled down the hood of her anorak that had constrained her vision and smiled apologetically. Caustic words stuck in Lyle's throat. Swallowing bile he could only blink, then reflexively smile back. She was young, her cheeks were flushing in embarrassment, her thick blonde tresses released in an unruly thatch could have made her an honorary Dutch girl. She ran her fingers through them to tidy and straighten. Her smile was broad, easy, disarmingly so.

'That's OK. I almost took you out though,' Lyle said. 'You were going to be my third American today.'

He had a speech all planned now, about notches on his frame, but then instantly thought better of it when he saw her face drop.

'I'm Canadian, actually.'

'Oh. Sorry.'

'From Winnipeg.'

Lyle could only shrug.

'I was looking at the street sign,' the girl quickly added, pointing up. 'I was trying to work out where I was.' She pulled out a map as if to make her defence watertight.

Lyle sought out the juncture on the map, mumbling, then

to his eventual relief with occasional glances up at the sign to reconfirm its name, found the spot.

'There.'

'Thanks so much. I was looking for the Anne Frank house.'

'Can't miss it. Just follow the trail of tourists.'

'Oh. You live here?'

'Yes. I'm originally from England, but I've been here for a few years now.'

'You're very lucky,' she said looking down at his rental bike.

'I know, I know,' Lyle said indulgently.

The girl tucked her map away.

What's her name? Ask her what her name is. Tell her your name.

'Is there a place to have a coffee and something to eat around here?' she asked. 'I want something before I follow the other tourists to the Anne Frank house.' She smiled at him. 'Would you recommend somewhere? Somewhere *locals* go?'

Now, damn it, tell her you know a place and you'll offer to show it to her and ask her if you could accompany her for a coffee.

'Well...' he started.

C'mon, you're not that stoned.

'Er...'

Now smartarse. NOW!

But he could not do it. Something stopped him from saying the words. Something implacable and resolute. Something he could not climb over or punch through.

'Er, I think there's a nice cake shop along this street you could try,' he said instead and vaguely pointed.

She followed his waving finger and smiled thinly. 'Thanks.'

Lyle watched her as she made her way along the street. She turned back and he quickly made an effort to look like he was examining his bike. When he looked back after her again, she had gone.

19/10 | Playtime

The Tacheles overseers said the photographer was a Catalan who came from an art collective in Friedrichshain and was only exhibiting there this week while the artist who normally occupied the space was away. They didn't have a number, just an address of the collective: my next port of call. The collective occupied a small converted shop front in another bijou district. A man appeared out of a dark room in the rear to tell me his colleague wasn't there, unsurprisingly. But he did know where he'd gone. I watched him scratch out the address with a stubborn bic biro on the reverse of a Chinese takeaway lid, a loupe swinging from a chain around his neck. He had bulging eyes and the cadaverous complexion of a man who hadn't been exposed to light for quite some time.

On to the address he'd written, which was nearby. Once I got there the photographer was not hard to find. He was lying on his back at the base of an imposing monument carved out of stone in unmistakable Soviet realist style. It featured a moustachioed face looking sternly into the middle distance, one hand raised in a fist, a banner in frozen ripple behind him. The photographer wasn't moving either, the hands to his sides, one gripping a Canon SLR. Pigeons waddled about him, heads bobbing in their incessant rite of ground pecking and courtship. Seeing him like that reminded me of the playful photographer in Antonioni's film *Blow Up*, but that character had slightly more animation. I watched for a couple of minutes and he still hadn't moved. I wondered if he was alright and went for a closer look. When I stood over him the only part of him that did finally move was his mouth.

'You're in my light,' he said.

I looked up and took a step to my left.

'Thank you.'

'Are you Pepe?'

The eyes finally moved to appraise me.

'Yes. What can do I for you?'

'You took the picture the Tacheles used in a poster promotion?'

'Yes.'

'I am looking for the woman in the picture.'

'You mean K., the butterfly? I haven't seen her in a while,' he said, loosening a red and white checked scarf from around his neck as if it was choking him. The scarf looked like the ones the Khmer Rouge in Cambodia wore.

'Do you have a contact number?'

'I did have, but the number doesn't work anymore. Disconnected.'

Dead end.

'Same here. How well do you know her?'

'No better than you, it seems.'

A pigeon swooped down across the plaza to rest on an outcrop just below the chin of the carved head. The photographer's camera with its long lens whipped up to his face, but the pigeon, alarmed, clattered off to take refuge in one of the surrounding trees.

'I'd appreciate it if you told me what you know,' I said.

He shrugged, which looked unusual from a lying position. 'Like I said, not much really. I saw her on a tram in Mitte. She has an… enigmatic face. Reminded me of the girls I knew in the barrios of Barcelona. Like she should be drinking absinthe in a bar in the Gothic Quarter. When she got off at Hackescher Markt, I decided to follow her. She went into a clothes store and I went in, too, and asked her if I could take some pictures of her. At first she was reluctant but agreed to let me shoot some rolls after a rehearsal that evening with the band she was in. We hung out a few times after that but K. is, you know, she's a… how do you say?' He shrugged again. 'I don't know… a butterfly.'

'The band. You remember the name?' I asked. Regrettably I had ditched the flyer for the gig I saw her at.

'No. But I know where they practice. It's on -strasse.'

'Thanks. I have to ask you something else.'

'Tell me.'

'The picture. It looks familiar somehow. The composition, I mean.'

'Picasso. *War and Peace*.'

'He did photography?'

'Not really. The shot copies a simple portrait he did of a lover.'

'I really like it. I'd love a copy.'

'I have quite a few of the posters. I'll send you one.'

'Thanks, I'd appreciate it.' I wrote my address on the reverse of a receipt for a German grammar book. 'I'll pay the cost.'

'No bother,' he waved away the offer with one arm that then took the proffered address. 'I don't like having reminders of her around in my studio. Too distracting.'

I looked at the monument.

'Communist?'

'Yes.'

'You know anything about the guy depicted on it?'

'It's Ernst Thälmann,' he said, pointing to the large carved capitals that wrapped around the plinth and were now covered with artless graffiti. 'Leader of the German Communist Party in the 1930s. He was put in jail by the Nazis and executed just before the War ended. This whole area was demolished and cleared by the Soviets for a memorial park in his honour.'

I looked at the grey monolithic tower blocks beyond, built as examples of Communist enterprise and was immediately reminded of the drab slabs in London, testament only to the post-war lunacy of certain borough councils.

I looked back down at him.

'Last question. Why exactly are you on the floor?'

'The light.'

'What?'

'I'm waiting for the sun to come round and shine fully on Thälmann's face.'

I looked up at the sky. He'd be waiting a while. I thanked him and left him to the pigeons.

19th October | 1945

I am glad the shooting and explosions and screaming have ended, but it is too quiet now. There is a gramophone up here and I desperately want to play it. There is no music anywhere anymore, and Grandpa does not even whistle like he used to. When he came up with cheese and bread today, I asked him if I could play the gramophone and he said grumpily that it was forbidden. They would hear. There is a record Mother used to play by her favourite actress, Lilian Harvey, who went to America. Sometimes she would sing her songs to me and we would dance about the room together as if we were at a ball. I miss Mother terribly and to play some songs would help me remind myself of happier times. I could dance with the mannequin and pretend it is her. But Grandpa forbids it. I know he cares for me very much but I hate being here in the quiet and the gloom.

At least I have lots of Grandpa's books to read, I suppose. He loves books, too, and tells me he even saved some that the Nazis wanted to burn before the war. They built a big bonfire in Bebelplatz and burnt thousands. How sad. All those words lost. All those voices silenced. I read all sorts and escape in my head to worlds I long to be in. Sometimes they are sad worlds, but they are still better places than this attic. How long will I have to hide up here? Grandpa says not forever, but does not say for how long.

I just heard Grandpa talking loudly to a man I do not know. I pressed my ear to the floor and listened, even though I know I should not have. I heard him say, 'Curse the Nazis for bringing this upon us. Packs of Russian dogs wreaking revenge on our city, roaming the streets for women. Damn this war to hell!' The man said something that I did not hear. Only Grandpa was talking loudly. He then said, 'I should not have had to have buried my son. He should have buried me!' He sounded angry, then sad, and started to cry.

I cried with him.

21/11 | Like dolphins can swim

The rehearsal studio was a converted walk-in meat freezer for a butcher's shop that was now a vintage vinyl store. After flicking through a stack of B's in the off chance of finding any LPs from Bowie's Berlin period I asked the guy running the place about my erstwhile singer and her band. He said a group that fit that description were rehearsing later that evening. Business was obviously slow as he was pretty talkative. We chatted about rare EPs for a while then I steered the conversation back to her band. He told me that another man had been asking about them a few days ago.

'Really?'

'Yeah, a scary looking guy. Asking a lot of questions about their hot lead singer. Said he was in the business. But that was bullshit.'

'You think?'

'Wouldn't know his way around a mixing desk. I didn't like the look of him and told him the band didn't rehearse here anymore.'

'I obviously don't look so scary, huh?'

'Well, you know your music, that's obvious. He wasn't curious at all.'

I almost forgot.

'What's the name of the band?' I asked.

'Kling Klang.'

I went for an afternoon run around the athletics track in the Mauer Park to clear my head, and thought about how best to approach the fact that I was turning up unannounced and uninvited at her band's rehearsal. Another question, though, grew more insistent with each lap: *What are you doing in Berlin? What are your plans? What happens when the money runs out?* The self-indulgence of my stay was starting to gnaw at me. There was little chance of work here, not with such diabolical German. So what was I going to do? Go back to London with my tail tucked between my legs? No. I'm done with London, another voice said. Samuel Johnson had said: 'When a man is tired of London, he is tired of life.' This was no doubt delivered from the relative comfort of his 18th century Men's Club in Soho. Cigar in one hand, port in the other, delivering bon mots in his wing-back leather chair to harrumphing Lords. Today's London would have him chugging back the port and on the next train out to a country pile. No, give me a city that lets me breathe, that gives me a bit of space, that meets my eye with a smile, not with a dead-eyed stare of confrontation.

As I weaved around various mothers in Nike branded running tights pushing their bawling newborns around the track I noticed another piece of graffiti sprayed on the side of an electricity sub-station beside it. Next to a large decorative tag a sage piece of advice winked at me in English each time I went round.

CAN'T KEEP RUNNING AWAY!
Too right.

I went back that evening and was immediately steered out the rear by the owner. I heard a familiar sound before I saw them but my heart sank when an unfamiliar voice kicked in. The band were going through their paces in a cramped space lined with foam walls, a cross-section of which looked like the inside of an egg box. I watched them dispiritedly as they played a rendition of Siouxsie and the Banshees' *Hong Kong Garden*. Their singer today was a slim teenage girl with close-cropped blonde hair with black streaks, a pierced septum and a reedy voice that hit the high notes easily. She wore a green t-shirt with cut-off arms that bore the motif for a band I didn't recognise. The musicians were aware of an onlooker and upped their performance, the singer tossing her hair like a Beatle mop topper, her left leg bouncing in drainpipe stonewash jeans in time to the beat, Converse trainers tapping the floor.

After they finished the track I introduced myself and asked the guitarist about their ex-singer. He was brusque and said they didn't know. While he explained quickly that she had quit suddenly without a real explanation, I was aware of the hostile stares of the other band members, especially blondie. They were obviously trying to move on without their Golden Goose and didn't like another reminder of their loss. Not only that but the bass player, the one who had introduced her to the band, was in a coma after a hit and run accident. I asked the guitarist if he had a contact number or address for her and he said no. Apparently her mobile number didn't work anymore.

Dead End.

October 21 | 1989

My love,

Last night I dreamt I was in a watchtower with Matze. It was night and a spotlight had fixed on a figure running to the Wall. Not to the border wall, mind, but to the backland wall on the DDR side. The spotlight followed the figure like an entertainer on a grand stage. I had the only rifle. Matze shouted "Shoot! Shoot!" I aimed and fired a shot but it missed, sending up a puff of sand. I reloaded and fired a second round. The figure fell to the ground in an awkward heap. When we went to collect the body I noticed for the first time the long hair of a woman. She was crumpled at the base of the wall. Matze turned her bloodied body over and laughed. Laughed!

It was you.

21/11 | Fear and dank

I can't find her, yet I see her everywhere. Gummed to sides of skips, pasted over existing advertising hoardings for telecommunications companies. Her eyes following me under bridges, over pedestrian crossings and up subway stairs. Every street corner, every available space she is there. Juxtaposed with posters for the latest epicurean event at the Kit-Kat Club, jostling for space with an anti-fascist demo announcement, vying for commuters' attentions with a Hollywood blockbuster (with German dubbing).

She is everywhere and nowhere to be found.

Yet it seems that I am easy to find. But initially not by those I want to be found by. I'll explain.

It started with a morning like most others thus far. A guilt laden start of a day. Café ennui, watching the spinning spiral arcs of young galaxies in coffee cups turning suddenly into the gradual slide of suds down the insides of glasses, like small scudding clouds, to merge into the slowly dissolving head of another beer. A quick snack under the U2 line by Eberswalderstrasse station followed before heading back to a cluttered bedroom desk and a mocking blank page.

It did not mock for long as the buzzer on the apartment intercom sounded. I presumed it was the Anarchist.
'You forgot your keys again?'

The voice from the street was not his. This male's voice was thin, abject and warped by static.

'I want to speak to her. Is she there?'

'There's no *she* here. Who are you?'

A quaver of emotion was filtering through now. 'I know she's there. I want to see her.'

'Like I said, no woman lives here. I think you've got the wrong apartment.'

'I saw you come in. Your name's here. I know it's *you*.'

'Who do you presume I am?'

'The guy who's *fucking* her!'

'Well, I'm certainly not going to let you in if you talk like that.'

'OK, OK. I just want to see her. Just for a second, then I will leave. I promise.'

'Like I told you, it's just me up here. If you don't believe it, come up and search the apartment. Fourth floor.' I released the building's door to let him in. The voice didn't fill me with fear, and when he appeared at the door my guess about him was proved right, as was my guess at which '*she*' he was referring to.

He was a smallish guy in a tight fitting army surplus jacket with a brown leather satchel slung over one shoulder. He had artfully sculpted stubble and a grey Panama hat that perched on rich brown curls. He was angry and nervous at the same time, his body trembling slightly as if in reaction to competing inner emotions.

'I saw you out together last week. You were carrying her,' he said straight away.

'That was the last time I saw her, too. Look, I don't know where she is.'

He looked down the apartment corridor as if expecting to see her head peek out from behind a door frame.

'How did you know I lived here?' I asked.

'You were at Konnopke's Imbiss and when you left, I followed you. I wanted to see if she was here.'

'Great currywurst there,' I said, trying to diffuse his tension. I was taking it calmly, which surprised me, and was grateful the Anarchist wasn't at home. One look at this gauche figure standing in the doorway would have been enough. He would have garrotted him with the strap of his satchel, before feeding him his own hat.

'She's not here and she is unlikely ever to be. I'm sorry to disappoint you, but you'll have to look elsewhere.'

'If you do see her—'

'Unlikely.'

'If you do, then tell her Dietmar…'

'Yes?'

'Tell her Dietmar would like his Herman Hesse back.'

He turned to leave, shoulders slumped.

'How do you know her, by the way?' I asked him.

He faced me briefly and said, 'I met her in a taxi,' before trudging back down the stairs. As I closed the door I couldn't help wonder who else she had spinning in her orbit.

A few minutes of staring at the wall and the buzzer went, this time to the apartment door. I opened it expecting Panama hat back to double check to see if I hadn't been lying to him. Instead a Turkish looking man stood outside. He was thick set with a slight slant in his posture, a shaven head with salt and pepper sheaves, and wore an off-centre smile that didn't go anywhere near his eyes. I had to resist a sudden urge to slam the door in his face.

'Hello, my friend.'

He was wearing a cheap looking polyester suit with smooth patches that caught the stairway light and a turtle neck sweater underneath. He possessed a face that can only be described as looking like it had been sculpted in plasticine by someone who had given up half way through.

'You and I have someone in common.'

'And that is?'

'I think you know who I talk about.'

'And who are you? Her stylist?'

'Where is she?'

'I wish I knew.'

'Why don't we sit down? It's better to talk, yes?'

'I don't know if I want to invite you in. You haven't told me enough about yourself.'

'Let me sit and I tell you.'

Against my better judgement I did.

He came in, sat down at the kitchen table and gestured for me to do the same, as if it was his apartment and I was the guest. He sat, straight backed, calmly observing me.

'Can I get you something to drink?' I offered.

'No, no. Come, sit. We have talk.'

I sat, he talked.

'I represent people who would very much like to find her. They are concerned for her. They pay a lot of money for information on where she is. We know you know her. You tell me where she is and we are all very happy.'

'How did you find me?'

'That is not important.'

'Did you spot me at the currywurst imbiss, too?'

He just looked at me with that crocodile smile fixed on his face.

'Where is she?'

'I don't know.'

He placed large hands flat on the table in front of him, a wide span that implied very little but made a bead pop out on my forehead. I hoped he hadn't seen it.

He dropped his head to his chest, examining me under straight black brows.

'Come, my friend. I think you know really. Tell me.'

Just then the sound of a key in the lock reached us and the Anarchist appeared with a bag of organic groceries in his arms. His timing was impeccable and I could have kissed him for it – even if it would have resulted in a fat lip.

The Turk casually eyed him up and down, evidently decided two was too much bother and stood up.

'Well, it was nice having this talk,' he said to me. 'I have to go now.'

The Anarchist knew something was up and stood in the doorway not moving, to such an extent that the Turk had to almost squeeze past him on his way out. Their noses nearly met, the Anarchist being slightly taller, but the man wasn't perturbed by the frostiness in the slightest and cracked him his slanted smile. The Anarchist merely eyeballed him. He'd seen a lot of trouble in his youth: rival squatters losing it on meths, militant Marxists, riot police, fascist thugs. He could handle himself. But this Turk had swum up from the depths. He was from the netherworld, and I hoped buttons weren't going to be pushed.

'Try calling first next time. We'll do lunch.' I tried to say this breezily.

He turned his smile on me. 'Sure, sure. See you around.'

The Anarchist closed the door on his back.

'Who the *fuck* was that?'

'You know the Lebanese girl?'

'Trouble?'

'Trouble.'

Lost Weekend | Mike

He could tell he was getting close. The streets suddenly were populated solely, it seemed, by men walking about by themselves. More often than not they were walking absently, as if lost or free of assignations. Hands dug deep in pockets, eyes shifting constantly, refusing to meet the look of the other. And if these were the frequenters of the RLD, they weren't what Mike expected. Sure, there was the sartorial inelegance of the awkward nerdy type, but there were also the suited and respectable types: the captains of industry, the college professors; who knows, perhaps a few politicians. Mike then remembered once jogging across Tooting Bec common at dusk one weekend and encountering a similar site: men of all hues and social calibrations wandering absently by themselves, as if lost in existential thought, unconnected, yet sharing a single purpose, a pattern in the seemingly randomness of traipsing about a London common. But, of course, there was a singular purpose – the overwhelming and all-consuming need for sexual gratification.

The same inexorable drive, the same primal impulse, saw the men in the RLD wander about the tightening streets looking for that girl that fit their fantasy lay. Were they lonely? Mike wondered. Were they unfulfilled in their regular lives? What propelled them down those streets? Was it the need for brief satisfaction, was it the marriage of enjoyment and necessity, was it for enjoyment without the pain of emotional attachment and commitment, a divorcing of the visceral from the cerebral?

That same pleasure principal, it seemed, drew Mike on into the district. He felt a frisson of excitement at the sordidness of what was what he about to see. A grammar schoolboy's dry-mouthed palpitation at being exposed to something illicit, frowned on, like the time he found a crumpled, slightly damp edition of a pornographic magazine that had been tossed into a hedgerow when he was twelve.

He joined the other ambling men, anxious hands firmly entrenched in his pockets. It was strange to go back in the daytime. He had staggered, doped and drunk, through the district with his mates the previous night, bug-eyed at the scantily clad women in the windows above the red-neon strips. There was a particular place he wanted to find, that they had stumbled upon in their hazy ramblings through the district. A run of narrow alleyways, barely wide enough at some points for two people to walk abreast. It was by a dope-selling bar… *was it the Bulldog bar?* He couldn't remember. But he did remember its outside was covered in artful graffiti. He passed a gaggle of Italian men laughing and showing the contents of shiny black bags as they stepped out of a sex shop. He was close.

He heard them first before he saw them. *Tap tap tap.* The three booths in the first alleyway to his left were occupied. Voluminously buttocked black girls in PVC outfits that choked rather than hugged their bodies were tapping their long, elaborately painted nails against the glass doors to get the attention of the passing punters. *Tap tap tap.* As if telepathically linked they seemed to notice Mike at the same time as he passed. *Tap tap tap.* One smiled at him, beckoning him in with her long nails. Mike dug his hands further into his pockets and looked away. She opened the door and cooed something at him before he passed the alleyway and out of sight. Mike found his heart racing and fought the impulse to turn back. He was here now, he countered. He might as well explore. He saw the graffitied café now, and saw a man duck into a tight alleyway beside it. He followed.

The alleyway was extremely narrow; he wouldn't have been able to stretch his arms out for touching the walls on either side of him. There were many men coming and going, making it an even more claustrophobic space, lined on either side by glass-fronted booths and red strip lights. As Mike made his way up the alley, brushing against the other punters, he glanced into the booths that had their curtains drawn back. In one a ginger-haired woman in her forties was slouching on a stool with her high-heeled boots resting on a sill, disinterestedly looking out, a whip and a dildo – the dildo over ten inches in length – hanging on pegs beside her. Next door to her a short, plump, dark-haired woman gyrated slowly to music he could not hear. The next few booths on either side were busy, their curtains drawn. Then Mike spied a slim, young woman no more than twenty sitting on a stool applying make-up in the next window. Her straight blonde hair in pig-tails, she was wearing the slimmest of satin hot pants and a Stars and Stripes crop top. She saw Lyle standing outside staring and smiled the briefest of smiles. She opened the door a fraction to speak to him.

'Hello?' she said with an Eastern European accent. *Hullow.*

'Erm, hi.'

Her head cocked to one side. 'You want to come in?'

'Er, how much?'

'Fifty. Suck and fuck.'

Such words said in such a cursory manner by such an angelic looking creature flummoxed him. And before he could work out what his limbs should do next a man in a suit brushed past him and whispered something to the girl. She nodded and he went inside. The girl drew the curtain without a glance at him. *Tap tap tap.* Mike spun round to see a slimmer, younger version of the women in the adjacent alleyway go to open her door to beckon him in. He hurried on. Most of the booths at the further end of the alley were busy and he walked out to a passageway that had also had a few windows, but was even more crowded. The gaggle of loud Italians were weaving their way towards him, pointing, gesticulating and laughing at the girls exposed in their glass cages. Mike turned back into the previous alleyway determined to get out of there and head to a coffee shop when the curtain to the booth nearest to him drew back and a man stepped out. He paid no notice to the punter, but instead to the female occupant. She was in her early-twenties, he surmised, long shoulder-length bottle blonde hair, a full figure wrapped in white lingerie, her height augmented by clear plastic heels. She looked at him, smiling, and left the door open. He went straight in.

'Hello,' she said amusedly. 'Don't you want to know what I offer, first?'

'Fifty?' was all he could say.

'For the basic, yes. Is that what you want?'

His heart racing, Mike decided he didn't want to know what else she offered, that if he thought too much about anything, he'd lose it. He fished out the requisite notes from his wallet and gave it to her. Noticing the slight tremor in his hand her smile broadened. After counting the money she asked him:

'What's your name?'

'Mi- Steve.'

'From England, Mysteev?'

'Yes.'

'We get many English here,' she said. Did he detect a hint of disdain in her voice when she said that? 'Especially at the weekend.'

Mike looked around. The booth was about six feet wide and fifteen feet deep, barely lit by red coloured bulbs with a divan on one side and a sink in the other. On the wall above the divan was a full-length mirror. He watched the woman's reflection as she clacked over the tiled floor in her heels to one corner and bent down to change the track on her CD player.

'My name's Jolander,' the woman said. 'You like dance music?'

Mike nodded. 'Where are you from?'

'Holland,' she said, standing up and wiggling her hips in time to the music, checking herself in the mirror before sitting on the bed. He watched, rooted to the spot.
She took off her bra then looked over at him.

'You want to get undressed? We can't do anything with your clothes on.'

Mike undressed mechanically and hung the clothes over a green-painted chair. She was naked now, bar stockings and heels, and beckoned him over. He was barely aroused but when she cupped him that all changed. He lent down to kiss her, but a hand went up admonishingly.

'Just suck and fuck. OK?'
Mike nodded and the smile came back. She had a condom in her hand, expertly removing it from its packet and sheathing on his now tumescent penis. After a few minute's oral, she turned over, exposing a tattoo on her flank that spelt out in a handwritten script: *Mohammed*.

Looking over her shoulder she asked him, 'You want to do it doggie style?'

Immediately after ejaculation there was clarity. It was as if the primal urge had thrown a gauze over the sub-conscious mind and, after satiation, that gauze was lifted. Mike had a post-coital epiphany of sorts; a lucidity of thought in the vacuum left by his sexual pre-occupation. He was aware of the total inconsequence and futility of his previous concerns, of a sense of emptiness, of the brief exorcism of a reptilian impulse that had possessed him completely. This was soon followed by a sense of guilt and shame that was more than just Puritanical heritage. It was, well, *feminine*. The woman, oblivious to the naked man on her divan and his abstractions, went about the business of preparing herself for her next customer: disposing of the condom in a three-quarter full plastic bin under the sink, swabbing herself with some wet wipes, pulling on her alluring garments, checking herself in the mirror – a dab of eyeliner, a slash of lipstick. Mike wasn't there anymore. He was post-coital and post-Euro. He was post. And once he was dressed, he was shepherded out with a smile and a steering arm that only compounded his despondency. The previous moments had been simply a transaction. Of the fluid and fiscal kind. *Well*, that lingering feminine voice in his head said, *what did you expect*?

He desperately needed a smoke.

21/10 | The loud Flash Crowd

At ten thirty that night the buzzer sounded on the apartment's intercom once more. I called out to the Anarchist that I'd get it, but this time I went to the balcony and looked down. I saw a figure looking up at me in the gloom of the street below. One hand was clearing black tresses from an oval face.

'I lost your number, but you left your address with the photographer,' the face said.

It took a while for me to say something. Eventually I said, 'Come on up,' as if I'd been expecting her. I buzzed her in and left the apartment door ajar while I fixed myself a shot of Bushmills in the kitchen. I heard the sound of boots on four flights of stairs before I saw her. With my whiskey I drank her all in slowly: tan riding boots sheathed in sheer black leggings, a black satin jacket cinched at the waist that had a hood with a fringe of fake fur, plus a black cotton shawl with tassels that cushioned a flustered face.

'The last person I let up was not so cute. And he was looking for you,' I said.

She didn't blink. Unwrapping the shawl from around her neck she said evenly, 'He found you.'

'They. They found me. Something tells me knowing you isn't going to be good for my health. You have quite a few admirers that think you and I –' I left the sentence dangling over the precipice.

'I'm sorry for that.' She looked edgy, yet she met my gaze.

I gestured with my glass. 'Drink?'

'I don't drink.'

'I forgot. Tea?'

'Do you mind if we go for a walk? I have to explain some things. I think clearer when I'm walking. And I'm sure you have questions.'

'A few. I'll get my coat.'

We went out onto the street, both looking about for figures hunched in parked cars or loitering in doorways, but saw nothing to alarm us.

I looked over at her. I didn't know where to start. Eventually I decided to ask her first about home. 'What's Beirut like?'

Her face softened. 'It's a magical city, you would love it. But it has suffered a lot. Christians and Muslims constantly at each other's throats. When I was younger, Beirut was like Berlin would have looked like after the war. The centre was a... what's the word in English?'

'A wasteland?'

'Yes, of smashed buildings. Bullet and bomb holes in the walls that were still standing. It was not a safe city. Then the Syrians occupied Beirut for a while before they reluctantly left. And for a while it got back on its feet. The centre was redeveloped but they kept the original architecture of the beautiful French buildings.'

'It was a former French colony, right?'

'Yes. There was still evidence everywhere of our troubles, including the remains of the St. George's hotel where Rafik Hariri, our former prime minister, was assassinated by a massive car bomb. But there were signs of hope, too. Then the bombs went off again.'

'The war with Israel.'

'In 2006. It was a war between Israel and Hezbollah, really.

They had launched a raid into Northern Israel and captured two soldiers. The Israeli generals said they would bomb Lebanon back 20 years, and they nearly did. My family has a house in the hills north of Beirut where we went to escape the fighting. We watched the jets fly over the city and bomb the Muslim parts in the south and west. We watched the big clouds rise near the airport – big columns of smoke blowing into the bay. We watched the Mullahs scream defiance on TV. It was horrible. As promised, the clock was being turned back. But people are sick of war. They want peace and prosperity. Beirut still feels like a city on the edge, but it's still a beautiful city. I love her with all my heart. She will never die, despite her flaws and her fault lines. She has two faces, Beirut, and I love them both equally.'

'You would like to go back.'

'One day.'

'But the reason you can't go back now can be solved. You should to go to the police.'

She turned to me. 'No. Don't. No police. Please. You must promise me, no police.'

'Okay. But I don't understand.'

She looked at her new mobile. I thought my time was up. Instead she squeezed my arm and said, 'Let's go to the park. I know some people who are going there.'

'Tonight?'

'Tonight.'

'Good idea, I suppose; safety in numbers,' I said, half joking.

A small crowd had gathered on the slope just below the remains of the interior part of the Berlin Wall next to the former BFC Dynamo stadium in the Mauer Park. The backland wall was covered in graffiti. After spray painting their multi-coloured tags on every square inch of available space they had turned on the concrete floor, which was littered mostly with empty spray cans and the shards of smashed beer bottles. K. told me the crowd had gathered there for a specific reason and for a specified time. She told me that they even had a title: the *Nasus Flash Mob*. It was dark and cold but the assembled throng were in good spirits, filled with alcohol and purpose. Soon a hush fell over the group of mostly young people as the moment drew near. They all faced west, looking out across the part of the park which occupied the space where the Death Strip used to be, over the dormant flea market to the glittering lights of the buildings beyond, and they waited. Then at precisely 11.11 p.m. they filled the night with a cry.

'Chris Gueffroy!'

The sound travelled across the gap, bounced off the buildings on the old west side and returned to them, as if emitted from another group who had also come to join in with their efforts.

'Chris Gueffroy!'

After an earnest pause another shout as one, in English, and another strong echo:

'We remember!'

'We remember!'

After that the crowd gradually dissipated, pleased with their effort, having carried out their instructions, off to bars on the nearby Oderbergerstrasse. I didn't know quite what to make of the whole experience, but she was happier now, chatting to people she knew from previous Flash Mob outings. A few lingered, eager to try out other sonic feats afforded by the topography of the area. As we left, drunken voices called out across the strip, a muted response soon returning to those dark outlines on the slope.

After a brief drink in a bar – I drank, she talked – we walked the streets for a while as a thin gauze of drizzle came down and glassed the scene before us. As we wandered the silken streets she pulled her hood up and had to turn her head fully to meet my eye. Her face was framed then by the fur with little droplets collecting on the ersatz pelt, mingling to gum some strands together. I wanted to rub her nose with mine, give my Inuit an Eskimo kiss, tell her everything was alright – even though I wasn't certain it was; even though I needed being told that myself just as badly.

'You can stay at mine tonight,' I said.

She bowed her head. 'I can't. Not tonight. I want to, but I can't.'

I wondered how many other plates she was spinning in this city. And I wondered which ones were losing their centrifugal force and threatening to topple into apartment stalking, bell-buzzing despair.

'I have your number again,' she said. 'I'll call you, I promise. I just need to sort some things out first.'

I escorted her to a tram stop. One soon came clattering down the street towards us. She drew her hood back and leaned into me. A kiss, a reassurance, a spin of the plate.

'I'll see you.'

'Take care. Call me at any time if there's trouble.'

'I will.'

She hopped on and took a seat to the rear. The yellow tram trundled on, bell clanging to warn people crossing the road ahead. She looked back through the wet glass to see me looking back at her and gave me a long, deep smile. The tram slid along rain-slicked rails to leave me soaking up the wet and the carbon fart of idling cars.

21st October | 1945

I dream often. Grandpa says it is all the cheese I eat, as that is all that is left. Some dreams are welcome, and when they are gone in the morning I miss them terribly. Other dreams are not so welcome. Some dreams force me awake, crying, calling for mother, even though, more often than not, I cannot remember what it was that made me so fearful.

This morning I had woken up, but still kept my eyes closed, not wanting a nice dream to leave me. I was in my bed in my old bedroom. My bed was soft and warm and I could hear the faint clatter of pots and pans in the kitchen and Mother singing. The smell of fresh bread reached me in my bed, making my mouth water, teasing me out from underneath the quilt. The sun was peeking through the curtains, making the insides of my eyelids a warm orange peppered with moving brown patches, just like a kaleidoscope. Eventually I opened my eyes, but instead of sun I saw the last dance of my candle and the dark brown walls of my prison. It was still night. Something had woken me up. Then I heard it: the sound of gunfire and crying in the distance. I pulled the blanket over my head and willed sleep to come again. But it took an age to find me.

Today when Grandpa came up with tea I dropped it, some of it spilling on my socks. The tea scolded and would stain them, even though the bottoms were already very dirty. Even Mother could not get them clean again! I got angry and screamed at him. He told me to be quiet. I cried and said to him I wanted to leave the attic. To make me calm down he said he would talk to friends about taking me out of the city. Then he said he would cut my hair short and get me boys' clothes to wear so I could come down, but even then it would be a risk, he said, because I have a pretty face and also the soldiers beat up the few young men left in the city all the time. I do not like the idea of cutting my hair short to look like a boy. It would take a long time to grow back. Longer, even, than the time spent up here in this horrible attic.

I hate it most when I need to go to the toilet and I have to use Grandma's bedpan. And then I have to wait for Grandpa to come before he can empty it. He takes it down without a word, although it cannot be pleasant for him, especially when he is balancing on the stepladder. But he does not say anything. I want to say, 'Thank you, Grandpa,' but I am too embarrassed and sad to say this. I am most sad when my bleeding time comes. Mother called it by the seasons. She would say, 'It's Spring, isn't it?' just by looking at my face. I don't know why she called it Spring, though. It should be called Winter. That is the worst, when it is Spring and I have to give Grandpa my clothes. But he says nothing, taking it down the ladder in a big bundle.

I love you, Grandpa. Thank you.

27/11 | Breast to chest

We agreed to meet at the next Flash Mob event – the security of group gatherings in public places being its greatest appeal. Told to be there by 7 p.m. at Alexanderplatz metro station we were unfashionably early, but it gave us plenty of time to speculate on the nature of the next get-together, which had not been specified. There was a great deal of speculation, too, as to the author of the instructions, which were always written in English and were always preceded by the words: 'Nitram Nasus says...' The most favoured was that it was a Buddhist teacher from the Prenzlauer Berg ashram. Rumour had it that he was a former drug smuggler who had had an epiphany during an encounter with a Thai monk. Was it him? I suppose we believe what we want to believe.

We loitered on a wide concourse, a sort of mezzanine space between the U2 and U5 line platforms, the walls and columns turquoise tiled, the floor a smudged marble with the look of TV snow. Standing under the low ceiling with its inverted glow domes, we listened to the distant rumble of new train arrivals, the ice hockey klaxon warning of imminently closing doors, the occasional squeak of protesting escalators and an echoing rendition of a Bach composition played by a busking cellist nearby. We watched the ebb and flow of commuters, noticing the odd hardy pigeon tripping through the throng, having managed to navigate its way into the catacombs in search of warmth and scattered crumbs. There were some morsels on offer here, dropped by careless commuters who couldn't wait to get where they were going and had briefly stopped off at a nearby food stand with its array of semi-stale buns and stewed coffee.

Soon others loitered with us, exchanging the odd knowing glance and smile. A tribe among the rushing herd. We waited with them, providing more obstacles for commuters with assignations to slalom through. Then another busker arrived. And soon another. And another. They were spaced about the concourse but didn't play; instead I noticed they gave each other conspiratorial nods across the steadily thronging causeway. Soon there was a disproportionate number of musicians and idling people. And then, suddenly, after the cellist had finished, with an unseen cue the motley collection of musicians started up in harmony. They played a piece by Strauss and some of the couplets in the crowd, self-consciously at first, started a slow waltz. They did a few half-hearted twists and turns in available space until the numbers swelled and the dancing became less self-aware as people lost themselves in the music. Singles made joking entreaties to other nearby singles and then those who were dancing outnumbered those who were not.

She turned to face me and took my hands in hers.

'Well, shall we join them?'

'Did you know this was going to happen?' I asked, warily appraising the dancers.

'Of course not. But it's another wonderful idea, don't you think?'

'Two left feet,' I muttered quickly.

'That's perfect,' she said. 'Because I have two right feet.'

I put one hand around her waist and led her as best I could, allowing to be swept up in the music and the positive energy given off by the laughing, jostling couples around us. Some had obviously done this before, others improvised as best they could. It didn't really matter how you looked, though, as long as you looked like you were enjoying yourselves. And most were. Two tall women in elegant clothes swept by us, leaving a heavy trace of perfume. It was only on second glance that I noticed they were men in drag. Every aspect of their body language, however, conveyed a detailed appreciation of femininity; they were only betrayed by the thick-set bodies they had been given.

As we danced about the concourse I realised that this form of dancing was infinitely better than the furtive bump and grind of modern dance floors, with its aggressive posturing and strobe lit exposure of gurning, sweat-filmed faces and underdressed desperation. This was more personal. This had more *soul*.

We got a rhythm going and glided eye to eye, then soon cheek to cheek, pelvis to pelvis, breast to chest, as commuters flashed by in indifferent haste or stood and gawped for a few bemused moments, wondering where the hidden cameras were. The musicians played on and we swept each other around under the low ceiling. I imagined that grand Soviet sentinel above, known as the Television Tower, catching the sudden glare of a searchlight, once used to seek out Allied aircraft, and now dusted off, its beam directed toward the orb that housed the tower's viewing platform. Transformed into a giant disco glitter ball it spun and refracted the light in bright square patches, spraying its fragmented beams down onto the faltering streets above us.

I noticed one face lingering on the fringes. A wheelchair-bound girl, no more than fourteen, completely bald. She was well-wrapped up but warmed mostly by what she saw. A bright beam of a smile lit up her face as she watched the dancers, lifting her upper body on the armrests and swivelling in her chair in time to the music. She nudged back and forth as if she was deliberating whether or not to spin and join in. The spokeless wheels were covered in stickers. Among them I recognised names of the latest bands, CND, a smiley, a USA flag and an unusual sticker that featured an old multi-spoked wheel, like the one in the centre of the Indian flag. She sagged into herself then, head dropping, as though convulsed in pain. I turned my dancing partner in order to get a better look. The girl's head lifted and I saw not discomfort but the tail end of a laughing fit written on her face. She looked up to her left and tugged the sleeve of a male companion not much older than her at her side. They shared a few words while watching the dancers that had her convulsing again. I had to admit, the monk – or whoever he or she was – was on to something.

October 27 | 1989

My love,

Sometimes I pick up broadcasts from Radio Berlin. I keep the sound down low and close all the windows and listening to it makes me think of you. Not just in terms of where you are now, but also it takes me back to that first summer together, when we met at the Free German Youth camp. Remember? I would sneak into your tent and we would listen to the rain tapping on the fabric. One day you dared me to steal the battery radio from our camp leader. My heart pounding I raced back with it under an arm to your tent, my plimsolls squelching in the mud, imagining how you were going to reward me. You pulled me underneath your blanket and we turned the radio on. Spinning the dial we searched for sounds from the West and listened intently to the crackle and fizz of the airwaves between official stations. Many of the broadcasts we happened upon were jammed by the big Soviet jamming towers, and all we mostly got was our own boring broadcasts and the 'beep beep' of beacons that we imagined to be Soviet satellites spinning though space. You slowly turned the dial and occasionally a voice came through the speakers, accompanied by alien music and we would whisper excitedly trying to make out what it was behind the hiss and sputter of the jammers. It sounded so far away. To us it was the sound of another planet.

28/11 | Holiday in Cambodia

Coincidence. Does it happen to you much? That random crossing of paths with someone you haven't seen in eons, for example: a few seconds later and you would have walked on by without noticing each other. Or those moments when your eye gravitates towards something relevant just to you that happens to be there the moment you look. That precise moment, seemingly, just for you. The jury is still out on fate, destiny, etc. for me. But some happenings are, well, just *too* coincidental to brush off.

Like this one.

It's morning and I have just shuffled into the kitchen to make coffee, not quite out of the shallows from a deep sleep. The Anarchist was one step ahead, at the kitchen table in his boxers and a Dead Kennedys t-shirt, reading the *Süddeutsche Zeitung*, a hefty broadsheet. I stuck my nose in the fridge to find some milk and then turned to see over his shoulder a small photograph from a column on the page he was reading. The familiarity stopped me, but it took a while to register just who it was. He turned the page.

'Wait a second. Turn back.'

'What is it? There are no cartoons on that page.'

'Just go back a page, will you?'

'You can read German all of a sudden?'

'No, I just look at the pictures… I know that guy. What's the article about?'

'This one? It says he's a Spanish photographer. *Was* a Spanish photographer. Found dead…'

'Jesus. When?'

'Let me see… someone found him yesterday. Post mortem today… suspected suicide. You knew him?'

'Vaguely. I met him when I was trying to track her down.'

'Did he seem suicidal to you?'

'He was lying on the job when I met him, but he didn't seem in a slit-wrist mood to me.'

'They usually don't.' He turned a page. 'Fascist fucks!'

'What is it?' I said, looking over his shoulder again.

'The NPD party. Right-wing. They are holding a demonstration in Berlin tomorrow, and there's going to be a counter-demo. I'm going. You want to come? It could get interesting.'

'Sure.'

'It's about time you got your hands dirty, Englishman.'

'If it's for a good cause,' I said, pouring milk into my cup of coffee. It came out of the carton slowly in glutinous blobs.

The Anarchist looked over his paper as I cursed. 'Organic milk doesn't last so long, mate. Time to go black.'

Lost weekend | Lyle

One of the stags appeared before him suddenly.

Mike?

'Give me a toke on your joint, Lyle.'

'Where'd you skip off to? Kane was waiting for you.'

'You can talk.'

'What does that mean?'

'Just give me a fucking spliff!'

'Alright, alright. I haven't rolled one yet.'

'Oh, for fuck's sake.' With that Mike stomped off to the bar to get his own supply. He came back with a lit joint and, after a few heavy drags, a question:

'Where's Kane?'

'Went back to the hotel to call his missus. Battery on his phone is dead. He's in a right old huff.'

'Can you blame him? Best man, supposed to be organising the whole weekend, fucks up the hotel booking then disappears. One stag crashes his bike, breaking most of his major bones. Another *mate* also pisses off without telling anyone.'

'Yeah, well, I was fed up with all the bitching.'

Mike formed an expression Lyle didn't expect to see then. It's one he had seen before, though. That open-mouthed, glassy-eyed look, like a toddler with its brain on standby mode.

'How much you think the girls in the red light district make, Lyle?' he eventually asked.

'Well it's fifty a pop…'

'I know *that*, Lyle. I mean, it's common knowledge, ain't it?'

'I bet they make a tidy sum.'

'Let's see, fifty Euros a go. On average, let's say, two punters an hour, although we've seen some in and out in fifteen minutes. So that's, if she works a full day, about 700 euros a day, three and a half a week and 14 a month. Bloody hell! That can't be right.'

'They do all right. Otherwise they wouldn't do it.'

'They're not forced to do it against their will, are they? It's not like England with the sex trafficking and stuff. It's all Kosher here. Legal.'

'Above board.'

'They don't look unhappy, do they? They just look… divorced.'

'Obviously need the money. Why you so bothered about the welfare of hookers anyway, Mike?'

Mike ignored the question, taking a sudden interest in the café's décor.

'What's with the Inca stuff in here? Why do they have to have such weird walls? As if we need any added psychedelics.'

'Speeds up the trip, I suppose.'

'It's those Italians again. Wankers.'

'Have you noticed that there never seems to be any Dutch people in these places? Just tourists.'

'Do the Dutch smoke?'

'Sure. Maybe they get their supply by other means.'

'I hate Bob fucking Marley.'

'Comes with the territory.'

'If my bird wore outfits in the bedroom like these prozzies wear, I'd never stray. Ever.'

'Yeah, I bet they could teach our girls a trick or two.'

'Ahh, that's better,' Mike said, smiling for the first time.

'Bad boy buying a pre-rolled.'

'I needed it. You think it's exploitation?'

'What is?'

'The Red Light District.'

'Yeah, it's exploitation.'

'I suppose, but you know who's really being exploited?'

'The hookers.'

'Nah, men.'

'Men?'

'Fucking men are, aren't they? Think about it. Our lusts, our urges and whatnot. Know what I mean?'

'Not really.'

'Think about it. We get horny, like, and the birds, the pimps and the porno men, they exploit it. Bleed us of our needs, our... money. We got dicks. Birds aren't the only one with a biological drive. You know, with babies. We also got a biological need.'

'The need to spread our seed.'

'Fucking A. To spread our seed. And they exploit that. They milk us, right? Right?'

'I never though about it like that.'

'Fucking right!'

They sat in semi-comfortable silence then, drawing lungfuls of sensimilia, sometimes giving each other big brother grins. If the others were in a fix, well, that was their bad luck.

Mike looks stoned already. Can't take pure hash. Lightweight. Tosser. Tobacco is banned but dope is OK. Only in Holland. 'We are the lotus eaters.' Why did someone write that on the table? An old man. What's he doing here? My God, how bright is his hair? His ginger hair. His fucking ginger hair! What is he wearing? Ginger man. Ginger Baker. Eccentric. Slippers?

Velveteen? Is that a word? How does he keep them so clean? Modern safari trousers, but with red ribbon fasteners and a… what's the colour … turquoise … and orange striped over-sized shirt. Visual pollution. It says, 'Don't look at my fucking hair. Don't. Please don't look. Look at my clothes instead.' The joint dwindles in size, the roach paper browns, blackens slowly at the fringe of the glowing embers and the hit is coming…

Dope   poet.

He's a dope artist, that one. Artisan. The way he rolled that. So many techniques. A stamp of your personality. Two-handed – sure. One-handed – hardcore. Puts the tobacco in one hand then the paper on top. Puts the hands flat together then turns them round in one swift movement then lifts the hand as if practising a magic trick and there… the open upended hand reveals the tobacco lined perfectly on the paper. Cool. The cushion moved. It fucking did. Is that Axle Rose? Sitting in the corner. No. Can't be. Why not? He's wearing wrap-around shades indoors. Very rock star. The face is a bit too… gaunt… though. Is he looking at me? Can't tell. Shouldn't stare. A little too thin. The hair a little too 'rasta man'. Dreads. Has all the tattoos and piercings you need, though, to be a rock star. Track marks? Was he a junkie? Could he speak Dutch? Doesn't he have a whiny voice, or is that just when he sings? What's that on his table? Soft Secrets. Dope grower's monthly. Mmmm. The music style seems to be changing every track, or have we been in here that long? Is time warping, folding into one law-breaking whole? Time is a false construct anyway. I read that. Listen to me! What a waste. Samba; sixties psychedelic rock – what a surprise. Ginger likes that. Nodding away, rolling his spliff (two handed). Now African boom boom music. God those girls are fat. Sit on my face, fatty! They'd suffocate you. Ska, now Hip-hop. Did that cushion move? Something is under the cushion. Fucking is.

Look! Don't look. I can't move. My lips. I want to look. They haven't seen it. Mike can't see anything now. I'm nearest. What should I do? Always three metres from a rat. No ten. In London. No five. Axel Rose is fucking staring at me. He fucking is. But I can't tell for sure because... He's staring. Right. At. Me. Maybe because I was watching him. Terminator. I'm not leaving. Can't. Look at the walls. The murals seem to be changing hue and shifting the more I smoke. The figures, their eyes staring right at me; there are eyes all over the wall. Were there eyes before in the triangles? Greek? Egyptian? Like the Rijksmuseum girl. Alive.

I can't. I mean, I don't have a lighter. Sorry. Eyes. She smiled. At the bar. But the smile wasn't in the eyes. She must have given me the wrong type. Divorced? Black Widow. God this is strong. Super skunk. Wrong dosage. Wrong. Wrong. Wrong. Game over, man. GAME OVER. Are they aware how slow and erratic/deliberate/slow my actions are? Now the music is Arabic. Its gentle... lament... is the most beautiful I've heard so far here. Not so bad place. There's a pulsing, a subtle caress of the temples; it seems like my head is expanding like the unfurling of petals in the fingers of light, teasing them open. I should write this down. Dope's Pope. I could be a writer. Why not? Classical. No. Classical intro. The song. My limbs feel disjointed now. Dis- dis- distended, gaining weight.

This is a ride.

I'm ready to get off now.
I feel like a puppet whose puppet master is stoned.
There is a time delay from the synapticimpulseofthought and command and the body receiving the instructions and acting on it...

DE-LAY.

Woah. Smart drug?

Where did Axle go? Axle Rose is gone. Axle Rose is gone. See ya, Axle.

Mike looks gone. Acting kind of funny even before the dope. We all
We
We are
the lotus eaters. We are the eaters of the lotus. Lotus. Eat. Lo. Tus. An old man. Man? Tran? Wo-Man. Fe-Male. What's he doing here? Why doesn't he go away? Go away ginger hair. I bet he'd like ten inches of plastic up his hairy ginger arse. A full mop of red. Black cock. Block cack. Gair hinger. He was a ginger man
and an avid fan

of psychedelic rock

and big plastic cocks

Cocks

I feel

the eyes are still watching. More eyes. Churchill's. What?

Lyle looked over at Mike who was out cold, slumped in the corner, threatening to slip down and curl up on the bench. He slowly stood up and leaned over to retrieve the still smoking spliff in Mike's fingers and saw that his eyelids were rippling where the eyeballs were frantically roving to and fro, like a cat under a duvet trying to find a way out.

Some dream, he thought. *Enjoy the trip to the greenhouse, Mike.*

The face looked agitated, and he mumbled something, something that sounded like: 'Suck and fuck.'

Despite the dope redolence in the coffee shop Lyle smelt a cloyingly sweet scent of cheap perfume on him. He smiled.

Naughty boy.

Lyle picked up the packet of dope and stuck it in his top pocket.

I'm not staying. Let Mike sleep off his exertions. I don't want to be around any of them anymore. Let them all wonder while I wander. I never liked any of you bastards, anyway.

28/10 | Rote radwege

By this time I had grown quite attached to the Anarchist's bike, a basic one speed that the city's postmen used to ride. He was happy for me to use it and I would go out most days and explore the 'Berg', along the interconnected chasms of its streets. Travelling by bike proved to be the ideal way to see the area, flat as the city mostly was, with its plentiful bike lanes. There was the odd teeth clattering foray down a cobbled street, but they weren't such a hardship. Many Berliners, I noticed, took to the paths to avoid the cobbles, weaving through the walkers without slowing. But I considered this impolite and stuck obdurately to the streets.

On this day I decided to head down into neighbouring Mitte and took the straight run on Brunenstrasse which went downhill all the way. On this stretch even this old bike could pick up a good speed, as long as you were careful to avoid the dual tram lines that ran with the road and criss-crossed at one intersection. I was just building up some speed, taking note of the Falafel joints, cafés and clothing stores that went past, when an A3 sized poster tacked to the side of a construction site partition next to the former Kapitalismus squat made me slam on the break pads and pull over. It was a MISSING poster and the face on it was someone else I knew, albeit briefly. It was the Panama hat wearing guy who had confronted me at the apartment. His name was Dietmar and, according to the poster, he had been missing since the 20th. That was the day *before* he had visited the apartment. I got that feeling you get when a plane makes a rapid descent. First the photographer, and now this. I took down a telephone number and continued down the hill, between the right-hand side tram lines in the middle of the road. Lost in contemplation I was only vaguely aware of the tram climbing up the hill from the other side. As it got closer, so did the grille of an old black Mercedes, edging into my peripheral vision from behind. That soon changed when the tram came close. Instead of dropping back, with an aggressive change of gears it drew alongside on the inside and then edged across to nudge me into the path of the oncoming tram. I hadn't been playing close attention and, by the time I realised what was about to happen, it was too late. In a split second I was veering towards the now clanging tram. At the last moment I twisted the handlebar and took a glancing blow off the front of the tram, which unseated me. With an ugly sound of crunching metal the bike went underneath the rapidly breaking tram. Thankfully I didn't follow suit, but instead careened along its side before faceplanting into the bitumen. The tram came to a shuddering halt. The Mercedes sped on down the slope. I had no time to note the driver or the car's plate, too dazed and more concerned in taking a quick inventory of damage done. One side of my face felt cheese grated and was weeping blood; one palm was gashed. My shoulder was sore and one knee was throbbing, my ripped jeans would now have fetched a decent price in one of the nearby boutiques and my leather jacket was severely scuffed. But mercifully that was it. Faces peered down at me from the tram's windows as I shakily got to my feet. The driver jumped out and together we managed to extricate the remains of the bike. I owed the Anarchist a new set of wheels, but judging by the look on the driver's face it could have been a lot worse. I looked down the hill after the Mercedes. That had been more than just a case of reckless driving. Faces stared out through plate glass shop fronts, café dwellers braving the outside tables looked on and sipped their cappuccinos while children peeked over the tops of denuded ice creams. All watched the man with the wobbly legs and mashed up bike and reflected on his lucky escape and how the morning could have taken a more unpleasant turn. I picked up the remains of the bike and hobbled home. This plate was still spinning.

28ᵗʰ October | 1945

Sounds I miss most (not in order):

Laughter, especially Mother's (I've forgotten how Father's laugh sounded). Birds. Singing. Schnauzer howling like a little wolf whenever we sang! Water running out of fountains. Trains whistling and puffing (at night).

Smells I miss most:

Tobacco smoke from uncle's pipe (strangely). Wood smoke. Freshly cleaned sheets hanging on the line. Soap. Mother's smell (especially on her neck below her ear). Shoe polish and leather at the cobblers. Freshly baked bread.

Food I miss most:

Freshly baked bread (not with cheese). Gherkins. Chocolate. Boiled eggs.

People I miss most:

Everyone.

Yesterday a butterfly merged with my dreams. I was at our former holiday home by the sea. There was a walled rose garden there. It was my favourite place. I was reading a book on a wicker chair, protected there from the strong sea winds. The chair was the one with the holes, the one that looked like it had been chewed at by mice. I was sticking my finger in an out of one of the holes as I read, making the exposed ends of the slats give off little squeaking sounds, as if the mice were still there, crawling all over the chair. Then my father called me. He sounded anxious. I called back, but he did not seem to hear me. I headed for the gate, but it was not there. It was just a blank wall. Then the wall grew before my eyes, higher and higher it went, towering up into the sky, lost in the fast moving clouds. It stretched away into the distance on either side, like the Great Wall of China. I could still hear Father's voice calling out to me, and then the wall transformed itself. Instead of stone it became wood, with interlocking beams that were dusty and full of cobwebs and crawling with mice. It creaked in the wind and showered dust on top of me. I woke with the sound of Father still calling me. It was not him, of course. It was Grandpa calling up to me from beneath the hatch. I could not answer him for a while.

29/10 | Goodnight white pride

'Get ready.'

We were on the train and on the way back from the counter demonstration and things were threatening to get nasty.

The demo had passed off peacefully. The sympathisers for a right-wing party, the NPD, had failed to turn up in significant numbers for their march and the notorious Berlin riot police had kept their batons to themselves. A march, a few shouted slogans and unfurled banners and now we were on our way back home. The conversation had unsurprisingly rarely strayed far from politics. I had noted that Berlin felt a far more politicised place than London and the Anarchist had said that was unsurprising given the city's recent past. I had suggested, though, that perhaps it was political apathy that had let in the Nazis and he had shaken his head and had explained a few things to me in his impressive English, which lacked the harsh saw-tooth diction that most Germans have.

'Apathy wasn't the problem. There was a highly motivated number of Communists in Berlin who wanted the workers to rise up against the Weimar Republic. Many ordinary people feared that. They wanted to see a strong Germany again, get off their feet and poke one in the eye of France for the humiliation of Versailles. National Socialism seemed to offer that. Flag waving and uniforms – they bought into the bullshit.' He pulled on his beard with sudden fierceness. 'I hate nationalism in all its forms – it's a cancer.'

'Hold on. The Anarchists have a flag, don't they?"

'Not the same.'

I let that go. 'I think the general apathy with our generation comes from a lack of faith in the system. We have no faith in politics anymore, no faith in the politicians who purport to represent us. No faith in our so-called leaders.'

'We have no faith, full stop. But many people want, need, to be lead, need to be told what to do, what to believe. That's why there is *Ostalgie*, the nostalgia for the East German way of life. Some people born in East Germany miss the certainty of their lives then; the comfort, the control. That's why there are cults and those silly flesh mobs that that singer drags you along to. We want the safety of groups; we want to belong.'

'You mean *flash* mobs.'

'I would call them flesh mobs.'

'Actually, I'm warming to these *flesh* mobs. But what you're saying is maybe some of us lack purpose in our lives, and look for alternative ways to find it.'

'Politics. Political idealism gives us that purpose.'

'Maybe,' I said, recalling what I had read about Bader Meinhoff. The idea of young people from affluent academic backgrounds committing murder – of shooting and bombing in the name of a political ideal – was so remote to me. Would that ever happen again among the white middle-class in today's western society? Would students kill in the name of politics? Probably not. I doubt many young people would canvas, let alone kill, for politics in our country.

It was then that the Anarchist noted some new arrivals in the carriage. Black baseball cap wearing youths in mostly grey and black garb drinking bottled beer, which was permissible on Berlin trains.

'Fascists?' I asked him.

'Wankers. See what's on that t-shirt the taller one is

wearing. "Goodbye left side." It's a right-wing statement against the left-wing motto, "Good night white pride." The others are wearing a brand favoured by fascists in Berlin. A brand called *Thor Steinar.*

'Do you think they were at the demo?'

'Who cares? All fascists are tossers.'

The Anarchist said this loudly, fists balled, looking straight at the group. There were four of them but he didn't seem to be thinking about the odds. I flexed my right elbow to see if it was better after yesterday's altercation with the tram. I had the feeling that I was going to need my favoured right. My messed-up face had caught the wary eye of some of the other passengers and I hoped it might help make me look more intimidating to these neo-Nazis. I looked at the seething Anarchist. For him there was little hindrance between the transition from thought of confrontation and the deed. For me there was a bit more of an impediment, but that palisade of general pacifism was about to be quickly breached.

'Get ready,' he said.

He shouted over to them in German and the group who had been laughing at something turned to stare at us grim faced.

'What did you say?' I asked.

'I told them, "Antifa is watching you."'

There was no time for more explanation as the one with the t-shirt in English stood up and said something to the Anarchist. The others in the carriage visibly tensed. The Anarchist casually stood up as if it was our turn to get off the train, but the train was not slowing. Then a half-finished bottle smashed on a rail beside us and the next moments were a slowed-down tableau of flailing arms, snapping heads and curses.

The Anarchist had felled the taller of the neo-Nazis quickly with a straight-armed economical punch to the nose and was now being set upon by the others. I entered the fray and deployed one of the few weapons I had in my arsenal – ducking a haymaker from a neo-Nazi I bent low and sent one shoulder into his mid-rift, wrapped my arms around his legs, lifted him off his feet and spear tackled him into the facing seats now hastily unoccupied. Another opponent nearby shouted 'Fotze' at me (one of the most unpleasant words in the German language) before delivering a blow to the side of my head which made one ear buzz. The force of the swing coupled with the sudden jolt of the train sent him sprawling forward so his back was now to me. Time for tactic number two. I thrust my arms under his and up to lock my hands at the base of his neck in a half-nelson. Using his own momentum I propelled him forward to clash heads with my first assailant who, winded, had been picking himself gingerly off the floor. The latter went down again. The youth in my grip, face now bloodied, flailed madly, cursing. I held on grimly. Presently the train pulled into a station. Many of the other passengers had moved on up through the train during the fracas and we were largely by ourselves. There now followed a temporary stand-off with both sides nursing wounds and trading insults. I noticed the Anarchist was grinning at them with reddened teeth.

'You alright?' I asked him.

The look in his eyes was febrile and euphoric. 'Never been better. You?'

'My right arm's useless.'

'We'll jump out just before the door closes.'

Soon a siren sounded and we bundled through the closing doors, leaving the neo-Nazis to scream invective and make threatening jesters at us impotently through the glass as the train pulled away.

The Anarchist waved them off before letting out a primal roar of triumph.

'Ha Ha! So long, fascist fuckers!'

My heart was thumping in my ears. My hands were visibly trembling as my body worked out what to do with a second shot of adrenalin in as many days.

'Just as well none of them had knives,' I said.

'This isn't London. Knife attacks are rare here, even by fascists.' He turned to me. 'Ha! Just look at you. You've been in the wars this week.'

'Berlin is not good for my health. I'll have to go back home just to get some peace and quiet. What did you say to them before things kicked off?'

'I told them the brand they wear was now part owned by an Arabic consortium. They didn't like that one bit.' Bright-eyed but calm now he gripped me on the shoulder and showed me his blood-stained teeth. 'Consider yourself officially politicised, my friend.'

October 29 | 1989

My love,

The gall of Matze is quite something. I don't know whether to be furious or to just laugh. Alcohol makes him so brazen. He comes in to our guard post full of smiles and jokes but I know it's the drink talking. I can see the tell-tale signs now. The glassy eyes and slow, deliberate movements. He even made a joke about Honecker, but the colleagues just chuckle. He's safe here and he knows it. He always looks at his copy of the SED paper, Neues Deutschland, *but he does not really read it. It's just for show, like most things he does. Everyone loves Matze. Matze the practical joker. Matze the sad little drunk. Matze my colleague. You know how I told you guards are put into pairs when patrolling the Wall so no-one will give in to temptation? Shows such faith in us, no? When we turned round at the end of our patrol section to head back today, Matze stopped me. "If I went to climb the anti-fascist wall would you shoot me?" I looked into his eyes to try and work out what game he was playing this time. "No, I would join you," I said. Cards on the table time, I thought. Matze is an excellent card player, though. His face never betrays his true inner feelings. "Let us go then," he said. "Let us go now. Come on, now is our chance! You lift me up and then I'll pull you up." "But the anti-climb pipe on top," I said. "Pah. No problem, come on!" And he started to walk over to the Wall as if he was walking across a park, not the Death Strip. I didn't follow him. He turned around and looked at me. "You are not going to betray my confidence, comrade? You are not going to shoot me, are you?" I didn't answer. I just looked at him. I had my rifle slung over my shoulder. I gripped it tight. I would not shoot him for attempting to escape, I would shoot him for being a shit. Eventually he just laughed his braying laugh and walked back to me. "You know, I would shoot you if you tried to escape. I would. But only in the legs. You owe me money and I need to give you time to pay it back." He slapped me on the back and we walked on down the column track.*

29/10 | Schönhauser Allee

'Oh my God, you look terrible.'

'Thanks. I did warn you.'

'And your flatmate?'

'Fine, apart from a dislodged front tooth that is killing him. He's gone to get some painkillers.'

'Fighting Nazis on the metro. My hero.' She touched my face with a cotton bud. We were in my kitchen. I was on a chair and she was standing over me, administering to cuts in a way that really was not helping. 'Did one of them attack you with his nails?'

'No, that was from yesterday.'

'What? You were fighting yesterday, too? I must speak with your flatmate. He is trouble.'

'No, no.' I reached for her hand that was dabbing my face. 'Listen, I have to talk to you about something. About what happened yesterday.'

'What is it? What happened?'

'I was riding a bike and I hit a tram.'

'Oh my God.'

'There was a car involved, too.'

Her eyes searched my face as her hands cupped either side. 'And…'

'And I'm not sure, but the car might have deliberately swerved into me to make me crash into the tram.'

'Oh merciful God. You think…?'

'Maybe. I didn't get a look at the driver. No police were involved and I didn't report the crash. But it's getting a little close for comfort.'

She pulled her hands away from my face and stepped back. 'I should not be here. I should go.'

'No, don't be silly. I don't know for sure that someone tried to kill me.'

'But they might have. I must go.'

'You've only just got here.'

She didn't answer and left the kitchen to get her things. I followed her.

'At least let me walk with you to the station.'

'No, you don't need to. I'm going to get a taxi.'

'I'd feel better if I could at least see you to the taxi rank.'

We walked to the nearest rank, which was opposite Schönhauser Allee Station, in silence. I sensed she was deliberating on whether or not to tell me something so I let her think. Soon enough she put an arm out to stop me and turned to face me.

'The man I told you about. The admirer. I was his lover for a while. He offered me many things for me and my family and I could not resist. I lived with him for a while until his ugly side became more obvious to me. He is a very jealous man. Possessive. I was just another toy for him, to go with his cars and his horses. But leaving was not so simple. He swore that if he could not have me, no one would. He has much influence in Beirut and he was true to his word. He swore that no-one else would touch me, love me – I was his and his alone. "If I can't have you," he said, "no one will. Anyone you touch, anyone who touches you, anyone who dares to get close to you – I will punish them. I swear this to you." I never thought he would send people after me, let alone carry out his threat. I should have known better. He doesn't want me back now, he just wants me to suffer.'

'Did you marry him?'

'No! But he has tracked me here and now… and now…'

'And now his henchmen are here. You *must* go to the police.'

'No! No police. It is not as simple as in the West. He has connections across the Arab world.'

'People are dying!'

'My family. He has threatened them. If I go to the police… my father, little Jemal, little Anisha… they are not safe from him.'

'Nothing can be proved… yet… but people you know are suffering accidents, dying or disappearing: the bass player, the photographer, the guy you met in a taxi.'

'What guy in a taxi?'

'The guy that wears a Panama hat. Dietmar. You have his Herman Hesse books, apparently. There are missing posters of him all over the city.'

'That's why I have to go. Leave.'

'But where? Where is it safe for you?'

She did not answer. She fought back sudden sobs but they came out in dry heaving gulps. I tried to hold her but she broke from my grasp and ran into the road, sending cars swerving, braking, the drivers angrily pounding their horns. She vaulted the railings under the arches and ran down the cobbled median strip, her hands furiously wiping her face. After skirting the stationary cars I raced after her and eventually caught up with her several metres down the strip. I grabbed one arm and spun her round. Her face was calm again, the smear of eyeliner the only evidence of a loss of composure.

'I am here for you,' I said. 'I care about you.'

She shook her head as if dismissing such sentiment. The

girders above us vibrated with the approach of a train. After taking a few deep breaths she looked at me and said: 'You must promise me something now.'

'Anything.'

Here it comes.

Lost weekend | Jason

The PVC gas mask spoke.

'You ever been fokked, English boy?'

He had not, nor did he ever want his holy of holies defiled – especially not by a faceless freak in bondage gear. But the point was moot. Jason would not be getting a choice.

The gas mask chuckled then drew in long, rasping breaths through its respirator. It sounded to him like a bargain basement Darth Vader.

Fucking fucked by Darth Vader!

The gas mask got close, examining him, cocked its head to one side then withdrew from sight. Jason could not see him but he could still hear him: the rasp of the mask and the slip and stretch of PVC on skin as the man moved about the dark, featureless room. Jason's head felt sore, and thoughts came through to him slowly and piecemeal; soggy croutons dredged up through a vat of chicken soup. It was like the after effects of a really bad hangover, but he hadn't drunk that much.

Somewhere above the dull thud of industrial techno sounded out once more. Jason struggled against the restraints again with all his remaining strength but nothing gave. He screamed something but the tape over his mouth buried the words. The mask snickered.

'You're going to get fokked, English boy. And then when I am done wis you my friends are going to have some fun wis you.'

Jason felt a hand on his bare buttocks. First a stroke, then a playful slap. He was tied, face down, to a massage table, his lower torso draped over the end, arms tied to the metal sides, legs pushed apart and tied to the rear struts. Primed and ready for plucking. To his right, on a wooden table pockmarked with cigarette burns and supported by two trestles, were an assortment of marital aids. Oversized dildos and other things he vaguely remembered seeing in the sex shops in the RLD, but couldn't, or wouldn't, put a name to.

Fighting back a sob he tried to retreat into a corner of his mind, tried to disconnect from the reality of his predicament, but the mask-distorted laughter always drew him back into the room.

'We're going to have some fun!'

Why the fuck is this happening to me?

The last thing he remembered was needing a piss and going to have a slash in the canal shielded by a tree. But the street was too crowded, so he had gone into a nearby bar to use the toilet. A fit woman with tattoos on her neck had started to chat to him on the way out. She had offered him a beer and he thought, *Why not? Amsterdamned!* Then after a few mouthfuls he started to feel more pissed than he thought he was and decided to get some fresh air. But he found his legs wouldn't do what he told them to and then she was holding him up, helping him out of the bar – and that's it.

His focus was dragged back into the room by the sound of a door opening and the equally unusual sound of another's breathing. Short and quick, though, this one. Sounded like panting.

What freak is this?

Then two masks came round the table to examine him. The black PVC gas mask now had a companion in freakery; this one had a white plastic skull you'd get for Halloween at any fancy dress shop. He'd seen one when looking for costumes for Kane. This skull had a prominent jaw with a downward slanting slit of a mouth, exposing an evenly spaced gap-toothed grimace. Wide eyes examined him through small rectangular eye sockets. Overall the mask looked to Kane a bit like a Stormtrooper's helmet from *Star Wars*.

Fucking fucked by Darth Vader and a Stormtrooper!

Gloating voices came out of the masks.

'I will be your first.'

Jesus fuck no.

'And Lars here will be your second.'

'Helloooo freshie freshie,' the skull said.

In one last desperate apoplectic fit Jason manically thrashed about. One restraint suddenly gave way, freeing his right hand. The masks backed off. Instead of reaching with his free hand to untie himself Jason went for the nearest available weapon on the table to ward off the gimp and the ghoul. It turned out to be an improbably big black dildo that made a passable truncheon. He swung it at them as best he could, shouting something incomprehensible, before working his left hand free as well, pulling skin off his wrist and one knuckle as he did so. The ghoul slipped away to his left but the PVC mask was at the table, looking around for something. Jason took this moment to wrench his feet free of their bonds. PVC mask was cautiously approaching him with a small brown bottle in one hand and a cloth in the other. Jason tore the duck tape from his mouth and with a scream that was part rage, part animal fear, upended the massage table catching the man on both knees with one edge, sending him crashing to the floor. Jason turned to see the ghoul clutching a golf iron, a sand wedge he noticed. In one corner was a small JVC digital video camera on a tripod. He picked it up and swung it at the ghoul, who with very little backswing caught Jason in the face first. But in his manic state it had little effect. Instead Jason's second swing connected sufficiency to send the man flailing to one side, the smashed remnants of the camera spraying shards across the room. The ghoul was hobbling to his feet so Jason reclaimed the dildo and beat him over the head with it, screaming something unintelligible despite now being free of his gag, before he dashed out of the open door. He was at the bottom of a flight of bare concrete stairs. He raced up them to another door with a spyglass set in it. He charged through that into a dimly lit corridor ending in multicoloured flycatcher strips. Through that he went into a comparatively brightly lit space. It was a sex shop. Men browsing DVD shelves looked round to see a wide-eyed naked man clutching a dildo. He stared back for a second, hyperventilating. To his left a fat man in a turtle neck was trying to extricate himself from behind a counter. Jason bolted for the exit, knocking over a life-sized cardboard cut-out of a porn starlet in the process. Out into the afternoon gloom he sped, looking over his shoulder for any pursuers, thus not noticing the rapidly approaching phallic shaped bollard near the edge of the canal.

29/11 | 40 per cent proof

I needed a drink. Fast. After seeing her drive away in a taxi I stopped off for some bottled pilsner at the local grocery store before heading back to the apartment.

Two flights up the staircase I came across a man in shabby clothes slumped over the balustrade. He was slowly sliding backwards down the steps, groaning. Putting down the beer I stopped his slide and looked up to see any possible assailant, mind racing at the various possibilities. The man turned a blotchy face towards me and said something unintelligible. A warm, spirit-coated breath met my face.

'Wie geht's?' I asked him, turning my face away slightly.

He murmured and tried to brush me off, only succeeding in slipping off the banisters. I helped him stay up and looked at the face set within a lolling head. Off-colour eyes, three-day stubble, skin blemished by a network of burst blood vessels and studded with open pores. He looked like he was in his sixties, but he could have been younger.

'Christ, you've seen better days, my friend.'

He seemed to understand. A smile formed. 'Ingss. Ingiss.'

'Yes, English. You speak English? Where do you live?'

He took in deep breath to compose a reply, an arm snaked up as if asking permission to speak. 'Nehba.'

'Neighbour? Mr. Smolenski? You live next door to us?' I said, realising this was the infamous Spiderman. I hadn't seen him before, despite living next door.

The arm that seemed to be on a puppet master's string now reached out and clasped my one free hand.

'Sulimsy.'

'Nice to meet you, too. Let's go upstairs, shall we?'

It took a while to negotiate the remaining flight of stairs and for Mr. Smolenski to find his keys, but eventually we made it inside his apartment. What greeted me inside was beyond anything the mind could conjure with credulity. There seemed to be no light fittings anywhere, so what little light there was that intruded into the apartment through the dirty windows mercifully hid the worst of the grime and mess. But it also helped conceal initially just what precisely constituted the mounds of junk that filled every available space. On closer inspection I saw that the majority of the debris was made up of piles and piles of paper. It lined the corridor that led from the entrance to the various rooms and filled the largest living space where we ended up. What little furniture there was in there was subsumed by magazines, newspapers, bound documents and loose leaf sheets. Nothing, though, could obscure a rancid smell that assaulted the nostrils and compelled me to put one hand up to my nose. Something with a sell-by date had been lost amid the mounds, or perhaps had crawled in between the piles to find a quiet spot to die. Looking around at the various heaps that filled every space I said:

'What is all this?'

Mr. Smolenski pushed a smaller stack of papers off a worn sheet-covered armchair and collapsed into it. The head lolled, and in an 180 degree arc the eyes briefly found mine.

'Dnke.'

'Do you want some water? Wasser, Herr Smolenski?'

The hand shot up seemingly of its own volition then fell back to his lap. Mr. Smolenski then laughed at an unspoken joke, shoulders shaking.

I went into the kitchen and was met with an odour that rivalled the smell in the 'living' room in unpleasantness. A plastic cup stood next to a virtually empty bottle of Polish vodka on a littered table. Its inside was ringed with a white dry residue as if rimmed by limescale or once used as a receptacle for toothbrushes. The only other mug was in the sink amid plates coated in orange slime and instant meal containers that now served as Petri dishes. I washed the cup out the best I could and filled it with water. Returning to the main living space I found he had fallen asleep. Placing the cup at his feet I briefly looked around the rest of the apartment. The bathroom I will omit to describe. There did not seem to be a bed in the other room that would have logically have been his bedroom. Perhaps it was buried under the mass of old junk and paper. I picked up a small stack nearest to me to examine. It was a jumble of typed and handwritten paper with varying typefaces on varying paper types; there were a few sheets of music compositions and what looked like dossiers full of typed reports and memos. I saw countless handwriting styles and different addresses on headed notepaper, too.

The oppressiveness of the apartment's stench was becoming too much.

'I have to go now, Mr. Smolenski. If you need anything just bang on the wall, okay?'

The head twitched and there was a faint murmur. I hastily left before I retched.

29th October | 1945

Today Grandpa only brought up half a roll. It was so hard I had to dip it into water to make it edible. It was mouldy at one edge, too. I saw the light green spot just as I was about to bite into it. I willed myself not to get angry or cry in front of him. I am so hungry, but I know he is as well. He looks so thin now, his favourite waistcoat hanging off him when it used to be snug. His face looks even more like an apple fallen from the tree, its moisture lost. My stomach is growling as I write. It talks to me, it says, 'Pumpernickel! Bretzel! Eisbein!' Another butterfly of a memory came to me then. I kept it and dwelt on it to make me forget my growing hunger. Playing detectives in the park when I was younger, with Gustav. He had the same name as one of the boys in the book Emil and the Detectives. *He called me Pony, another character's name, and we followed men who were strolling through the park by themselves. We pretended they were the culprits who had stolen seven Marks from us. One spotted us following him and had turned on us, waving his ebony walking stick. We had run from him, laughing, through the park back to my house. Grandpa said Erich Kästner, the author, had had his books burnt at Babel Platz. Why would anyone want to burn a book for children?*

When I was washing in the porcelain bowl that Grandpa brings up to the attic I noticed a new cobweb in the corner. I don't mind spiders and found this web to be beautiful. It

138

formed a perfect pattern between a wooden beam and the lamp stand that has lost its shade and stands on a box. The web was so neat. I remember reading about a Scottish prince and a spider. It convinced him to leave the cave where he was hiding and fight the English, who were chasing him. I wish I could leave my cave, but Grandpa always says the same thing. It is for my own good, and that it is not forever. But how long is not forever? I pray at night before bed and ask God to make the soldiers go away. But does God listen to people in dingy attics as well as churches? Before I go to bed I shine the candle close to the web, careful not to shrivel it up in the flame like I have done before, and say good night to the spider hiding somewhere. I wish I was as patient as the spider and as brave as the prince.

04/11 | We don't need no thought control

She's off the radar again. No call, no text, no reply. It's been a week. I think the worst but stick to my promise. No police. As to the other promise I made to her? Well… What did I feel for her? Could I cancel out my feelings? What is love anyway? What is it, apart from an overused noun, a trite sentiment rendered bland by ubiquity in pop-culture? It was deeper, more intense, more complicated than that. I suppose I could promise not to fall in love – but I couldn't promise not to feel. I kept saying the word out loud as I walked along the street, as if articulation and repetition was the cure, as if it would banish sentiment and exorcise the ghost of her from my thoughts.

Love. L-o-v-e. A consonant, a vowel, a consonant, a vowel. Love in a mirror evolves. Love: a drug whose dealer forgets your debts.

Speaking of drugs, the Anarchist had asked me to pick up a prescription of painkillers at the chemist. That's where I was heading. He had managed to grab the sole pool table at the local bar and didn't want to relinquish it. 'Besides,' he'd told me over the phone, 'it will give you a chance to practice your non-existent German, you lazy Englishman.'

I crossed a side street and noticed a car driving up the road behind me surprisingly slowly. It was not a Mercedes but my frayed nerves would not let me dismiss it, especially as I briefly caught sight of the two Arabic looking occupants in the front seats. I walked on for a few metres before stopping at what looked like small design firm, pretending to be interested in the displayed notices inside. The glass front of the office offered a decent reflection of the street behind. Ignoring the curious looks of those working within I waited for the car to pass. It didn't. I looked around to see the car was not there. Nor had it parked in a spare space by the kerb. It must have turned at the intersection, I thought. I doubled back for a while before hastily carrying on.

I found him in the back room of the bar where the pool table was. One wall was covered in a mural depicting an idyllic beach scene. A man relaxed in a hammock, arms crossed behind his head, straw hat tipped forward. Feet up, the pink soles pointed towards the table. The Anarchist was in the process of racking up for another game. 'Where have you been?'

'I had to do some extra things.'

'You get the drugs?'

I patted my coat pocket. 'Yeah. There was a bit of confusion at the counter, but I muddled through.'

'Thanks mate.'

'You're not going to take one now, are you?'

'With a beer? No. What do you want?'

'Weiss bier, bitte.'

'Your turn on the table. You've met Chris before, haven't you?'

I offered my hand to the man holding the cue at the table, realising too late that it was the only hand he had.

'Sorry. Sure I remember. We all went to that industrial techno party in Friedrichshain. God that was heavy.'

He took the opening shot, comfortably playing by resting the cue on the edge of the table and pressing the wrist on top of the shaft to hold it in position. 'Yeah, there was that scary woman in the PVC top who kept dancing close to you. The one with the bad B.O.'

I watched the smack and spread the balls as he broke. Two down. A stripe and a spot. 'Trying to forget. Always waving her arms about; that didn't help. God she stank.'

'That basement was a sweat box. I prefer ska nights at Ying and Young.'

He had a soft West Lothian accent and spoke impeccable German. He was married to a Berliner, mind, and had worked in the British Embassy in the city for over five years.

'I put some feelers out at the Embassy,' he said, lining up another shot. 'No work, I'm afraid.'

'No worries. Thanks for asking, anyway.'

'Have you considered doing a German language course? It would help a lot.'

The Anarchist was back from the bar with a round of beers.

'He's too bloody lazy. You're not going to get a job if you don't speak the language.'

'I know that. It's just that I don't know how long I'm going to stay in the city.'

'He can't take the pressure. What with dealing with psychotic women, crashing into trams and fighting fascists.'

'Yeah, I heard about the dust-up on the metro.'

'He's a one-man riot.'

'I was a pacifist before I moved in with you.'

My flatmate smiled. 'How does that Pink Floyd song go… "And did you exchange a walk-on part in the war…"'

'"…for a lead role in a cage."'

'Should be the other way round. And to think pacifists avoiding military service used to come to West Berlin.'

'How's that?'

Chris missed a canon to a corner pocket. 'West Berlin was the only part of West Germany to be exempt from National Service. Loads of students came here to escape.'

'He came here to escape, too, didn't you, Sassenach? And he found big trouble instead.'

My turn at the table. 'Sassenach? I suppose you leaned that off Chris, did you?'

'It's his new favourite word.'

The Anarchist looked down at the table. 'I love it. I love your expressions as well. You have so many. You said one the other day that I like: "Bust a gut". That's great! To struggle.'

'Well, to work hard.'

'You're not busting a gut the moment are you, Sass?'

'You can't talk. Your teaching career isn't exactly taking off.'

'Only Catholic schools are advertising round here, and Catholic schools don't employ atheists.'

'You shouldn't be so up front and honest. Just tell them you're a lapsed Catholic at interviews. And don't mention your politics.'

'Lapsed Catholic? And what do I do at morning service? Get on my knees and cross my fingers?

'Your shot,' Chris said.

My phone rang and I missed an easy pot. I looked at the display. Guess who?

I handed my cue over. 'I have to answer this. You take my shot.'

I answered, walking outside as I did so. 'Hello.'

Her voice was upbeat, peppy. 'Hi, how are you?'

'Fine. I was getting concerned.'

'Really? I'm okay.'

'No nasty looking Turks on your doorstep?'

'No, I moved to a new place. They won't find me here.'

'It's nice to hear your voice.'

'I didn't think you wanted to see me again. Not after what I said.'

'I thought the same thing.'

'Don't be silly. Of course I want to see you again. You want to see me?'

'With an armed escort, yes.'

'Sorry?'

'Bad joke. When?'

'Tonight. There is a fun event my new friends are holding. In Kreuzberg. You should come.'

New friends?

'Sure. What time?'

'Meet me at the Franz Mehring Platz on Pariser Kommune at six. We are going to see something first.'

'It's not another Flash Mob event, is it?'

'No. That's gone quiet. We haven't had a message from Nasus for over a week.'

'Okay. See you there.'

'Bye.'

When I got back to the table a new game had started and the two were laughing over something Chris had said.

'I still think the Ghanian High Commission was your best Embassy party story,' the Anarchist said to him before turning to me. 'He gets to go to all the parties held by the different embassies. I keep dropping hints for invitations but for some reason he ignores them.'

'You wouldn't come. You'd think it was all too bourgeois. And as for the concept of nation states... I was invited to one tonight held by the U.S. Ambassador.'

'It doesn't get bigger than that.'

'Not so raucous as the smaller events, though, and this was a fund raiser for a leukaemia trust. But it's been cancelled.'

'That sounds like it wouldn't have been much fun.'

'Not really. But a worthy cause. It was for his daughter who's been sick for some time, but she has obviously deteriorated. The girl is quite the celebrity on the Embassy circuit, whizzing around in her wheelchair at various events and organising charity functions. Bumped into me a few times.'

He showed me the small badge he had pinned to the v-neck jumper he was wearing, tapping it with his stump. The badge comprised of a picture of what looked like a potter's wheel with the words, *The Susan Martin Foundation* wrapped around its edge.

'I've seen that logo before somewhere,' I said.

The Anarchist cursed as the white went in. 'Your turn, Sass. And your round.'

November 4 | 1989

My love,

My parents have finally been granted an apartment in one of the new tower blocks in Hohenschönhausen. And guess what, it is exactly the same as your Uncle's apartment! The same dimensions, the same order of rooms in exactly the same configuration. I could walk around it blindfolded. My parents are ecstatic, but I cannot stand the low ceilings and fresh linoleum smell in the corridors. I prefer our building with its detailing, its character and its history. It may be drab and run down but at least it is not a boring slab. It is missing one thing, though; one important feature that it would make a perfect place to live.

Can you guess what it is?

04/11 | Die Büchse der Pandora

Pariser Kommune is just off Karl-Marx-Allee. A fascinating if somewhat soulless stretch, Karl-Marx-Allee was the showcase street the Communist Party built to have their May Day parades. It is easy to imagine the SED leaders on a platform somewhere on this broad stretch, waving woodenly at passing workers with their flags and red banners emblazoned with party slogans about solidarity, followed by flawless ranks of high-stepping soldiers and belching tanks. A procession of the party faithful going down the wide boulevard flanked by the imposing stately buildings where most of the party apparatchiks lived. The street was an architectural taunt: *Look at this, West Berlin. In your face!* It would not look out of place in Moscow or Kiev and made you feel you had somehow managed to instantaneously pass through a portal in space and time.

She was not where we agreed to meet. I took up an obvious spot and enjoyed a bout of people watching. I soon noticed a man in his forties loitering across the road, smoking a cigarette. He was wearing a suit but also an incongruous black beanie and kept putting one hand inside his open jacket without retrieving anything. I was wondering whether or not to move somewhere else when I felt something press into the small of my back.

'Don't move.'

If the voice that had said this had not made such a poor

attempt at imitating a hard man's voice I would have probably involuntarily loosened my bowels on the spot. As it was I spun round and grabbed the wrist that was holding a microphone with the base pointing out.

'Christ, you scared the life out of me!'

She merely smiled at me.

'What are you doing with that?' I asked.

'Protection. No, seriously, it's for tonight.'

'Are you going to sing?'

'No, a friend is. I borrowed it for her. Theirs is faulty.'

I stared at her. 'Wow, that's some haircut.'

It could have come out better, but she had quite a dramatic new look. She gave me a twirl, jerking her head one way and then the other. 'Like it?'

Her new haircut tickled a memory, a snagged synapse that took too long to work itself free and up to the surface of my consciousness.

'You remind me of someone else now.'

'Louise Brooks, perhaps,' she said.

'Who?'

'Caprice said I looked a bit like a silent movie star – an American who made her best films here in Berlin. She said I could really look like her if I let her cut it this way.'

I wondered if this silent film star had the same beguiling eyes and carefree sensuality, and how many besotted actors and directors she had left in her wake.

The hair had been styled into a helmet that hugged the sides of her face, the profile a vivid comma with a broad curve at the sides that swept forward to a tapered tip to touch the cheekbone. Brutally short but disastrous as a means of disguise as not only was it still coal-black but drew attention even more to her unmistakable face. Her hair was so shiny and straight it looked like lacquered vinyl. I glanced over to the other side of the street. The man I had noticed there was gone.

'I don't think it quite works as a disguise.'

'I've got a hat and sunglasses for that,' she said, grabbing my hand. 'Come on.'

She skipped up the steps of a Communist era building that looked like it had once served some official function.

'Nitram says, "Every day should be a challenge. Every day should be different. And if difference is not there – find it."'

'I thought you said-'

'It isn't. This is something I've found myself.'

I followed her inside wondering what small wonder awaited in this building. The interior was suitably utilitarian and antiseptic. We headed past the reception and down one broad bare corridor. She soon stopped by one egress and turned back to me to see the reaction on my face. In the small space inside I saw perpetual movement. It was an exposed lift, but like nothing I'd seen before. Imagine a series of coffin-sized spaces appearing one after the other, rising up slowly through the building on one side, and descending on the other. At each floor there was a similar aperture exposing this conveyance and into which you could step. But they did not stop moving; there were no stop buttons, no floor buttons – there was no need – so you had to step in at the right time and make sure all extremities were clear of the opening before you were carried up to the next floor.

'You first,' she said.

'I thought you might say that.'

I paused, looking at the succession of rising rectangular boxes, wanting to make sure I timed my entry right, slightly unnerved by the mocking metallic sounds of working machinery. Three, two, one... I was in. I turned to put my back to the rear of the mini-lift and watched the ceiling slowly sink and the gap close.

'I'll see you on the fifth floor,' she shouted through the closing space. I was then presented with moving bare walls an arms' distance away, but it was not long before another gap appeared and the carpeted floor to the next level. As I continued up I pictured each floor full of soberly dressed East German bureaucrats clutching dossiers on potential subversives, a few patiently waiting their turn in the moving coffins to take them to another department. I quickly stepped out at the fifth, tripping on the dropping floor. No one was about on this level either, but I did hear the screech of an audio track being rewound a few doors down – the sort of thing you would hear in a film editing suite. I waited for her. And waited. Had she lost her nerve? Had something happened? I considered taking the stairs down but then in the next box I saw the top of a head, then a solemn face, eyes closed, revealing silver painted eyelids. She had crossed her hands over her chest in a regal repose, leaning back, legs and feet straight together.

'Bing bong, fifth floor,' I said.

Without opening her eyes she said, 'See you on the eighth.'

As I soon discovered, there was no eighth floor.

Lost weekend | Mike

He was inside the booth again. But there was no woman in the booth. Just him. He looked down at his legs. They were slim and bare and on his feet were Perspex heels with rolls of dollar bills inside like prehistoric insects caught in amber resin. Was he dreaming? His nails were painted. Purple. They looked nice. He looked out through the glass of the door and saw it all now. Sadness first. Sadness in the eyes of the punters; sadness in the eyes of the tricks opposite. A quiet desperation and a soul-eating compulsion. He saw it all in the eyes that would occasionally catch his. Bitter, shameful eyes. In the eyes of the other girls he saw stoned vacuity, mischievousness, business-like bluntness and resignation. But sexually charged? The face, like an extra layer of make-up foundation, was prepared well in advance of the red-lit strip light going on and the crimson curtain drawing back. It was a face for the passing male throng. He drew the curtain closed. *Prepare a face for the faces you will meet, girl. Put on your act, put on your money-making performance – a smile here then a groan there – buy yourself somewhere inside and only let yourself out when the curtain is drawn closed for the last time. And don't come out for an encore.*

He drew the curtain back and was immediately presented with a punter. A small young man with ferret eyes and a sallow face. Stoned. Not good. He was being pushed towards the door by a group of laughing males of roughly the same age.

The young man smiled at Mike shyly as he opened the door. After more goading the man came in and was given a roar of approval from his leering friends. Mike closed the curtain.

'You're cute,' the young man said running his eyes over Mike's body.

Mike tried to project calm and went over to her CD player to put on some music. 'Thank you. What's your name?'

'Tre- Steve. What's yours?'

'Mike.'

'How much?'

His thrusting body on top was heavy and suffocating, as was his odour: an unholy melange of garlic, sweat and alcohol. His grimy hands groped and explored, encountering minimal defence. His tongue, slug-like, left a slimy wake on taut, cold, milk-coloured skin.

Over the sound of the man's grunting exertions Mike could hear the CD was stuck. A perverse thought crept into his head, considered that the stutter of the music and the singer's frozen contralto, as if doing warm-up voice exercises, were almost in rhythm to the man's efforts on top of him – if he just speeded up a bit. If he speeded up he'd be finished sooner, too. That would be good. Mike could also hear sounds from outside: a delivery truck's revving, inching up the narrow street; laughter from the man's colleagues, shouting for him to hurry up.

The man's jacket was draped over the solitary chair with its flaking green paint that exposed the red of a previous coat underneath. The young man's black socks were beneath the chair, looking like deflated balloons on the cold tiled floor.

Eyes closed he seemed totally lost in his efforts that pushed them incrementally along the bed. Some mother's son. Mike bit his lip and his mouth filled with blood, its copper tang reminding him of what would happen if he resisted his lover Mohammed's request again. He could feel the man soften, his ardour dampened by the dope, no doubt, only to regain tumescence when he redoubled his efforts. Mike felt a jagged pain of an old tear below grow more insistent, but tried to ignore it, ignore everything that was happening to him down there. He tried to retreat into himself, find a space in his mind, a dark tight corner, and curl up and wait for it to be over. A small voice in his head told him this was just a dream, just the fabrication of a fevered mind, and he could wake up if he wanted to. But the sound of the stuck CD brought him back, and his eyes drifted to his left, over the bobbing tangle of the man's greasy hair, to where the CD player was. He could reach it if he stretched out his arm. The button to skip the track. He could just about reach it...

04/11 | Queen of the underground

'Mmm. Handsome boy. We approve!'

I was being appraised by two men in drag. Silk gloved fingers rested on foundation-clogged chins and then occasionally flapped in the air to emphasise carefully considered opinions. Behind them the props to a finished stage show were being removed and a small plastic barrel full of numbered white balls was being wheeled in on a silver drinks trolley.

We were sitting on a table close to the stage of a small ballroom. The lighting provided by original chandeliers was low but I could make out the ornate stucco and rows and rows of black and white photographs, mostly portraits, on the walls. The ballroom was full of people facing the stage, sitting around square tables covered with white tablecloths. A very tall man in drag was tottering from table to table in pencil-thin heels exchanging pleasantries and handing out pieces of paper and felt-tip pens.

We had been joined by her new flatmates, Stella and Caprice, who had just finished their performance. The act had been rapturously received by the packed house and they were still basking in the afterglow of acclaim.

One of Stella's gloved hands reached out to cup K.'s chin.

'I love the new look. Caprice, darling, you have outdone yourself.'

Caprice wagged a gloved hand at Stella.

'Oh, I know. It's my best work yet.'

'She looks so divine,' Stella said. 'You look like a film star!' She then turned to me. 'Consider yourself a very lucky young man.'

'I do.'

K. gave my knee a squeeze under the table then stood up.

'Excuse me, girls.'

Stella and Caprice watched her go briefly before sharing a glance. Something unspoken had been exchanged. They turned to me. Time, it seemed, for the interrogation.

'What are you doing in Berlin, sweet?'

'I often ask myself the same question.'

'Well, what are you looking for?'

'I'll tell you when I find it.'

'Come, don't be like that! We won't bite.'

'At least not on the first date.'

Stella's Adam's apple bobbed as she laughed, playfully slapping Caprice's shoulder.

'Be-have. K. tells us you're a writer.'

'I write. I don't know whether I can call myself a writer yet.'

'The English have always been drawn to Berlin.'

'I know what he's here for. It was the same for Bowie and Isherwood and Cave and Iggy-'

'Cave is Australian, darling, and Iggy was American.'

'*Was*? Is Iggy dead, dear?'

'Oh I don't know, but he should be.'

'It's the same for all the male artists who come here.'

'I wouldn't put myself in the same bracket as them,' I said.

'Neither would I. Take Bowie. He was a genius! An artist.'

'A performance artist-'

'But they are both men. Men with creative impulses. They all want a muse, something to get the sap rising-'

155

'She will certainly do that for him-'

'She'll give him that. But you must give something in return, my dear-'

'A relationship is never a one-way street, darling.'

'And watch out, sugar, she's street smart.'

'Berlin was his muse,' Stella said.

'Who, darling?'

'Bowie.'

'That and the drugs and Romy Haag.' Caprice pointed over to one of the black and white photographs on the wall. 'She was Berlin's muse of the underground – in the seventies.'

'She was a performer in the Schöneberg clubs. He idolised her.'

'Berlin was his muse, too.'

'It's certainly a captivating city,' I said.

'She's a bitch sometimes.'

'Romy?'

'No, Berlin.'

'I wouldn't say that. She can be little cold. But she's been through a lot.'

'She's a tough, self-reliant maiden with a history,' Caprice said.

Stella nodded. 'She's made mistakes. She's suffered. But she is a better person for it. Deeper-'

'And more attractive because of it,' Caprice added. 'For those who know what to look for.'

Their toying with metaphor was interrupted by the tall tottering compère. We each got a pen and a printed sheet of paper with numbers in boxes on it. I saw K. returning and stood up to make use of the toilet facilities. 'My turn,' I said. It would give them an opportunity to pass on the results of their brief inquisition.

'Hurry up, love. The bingo is about to start,' Caprice called out after me.

On the way to the Gents I stopped to examine the photo of Romy Haag on the wall. She was an attractive looking woman with voluminous black hair and a round face. At least she looked like a *she*.

Was there a toilet in Berlin that wasn't covered in graffiti? At least most of the bits in English were cogent.

I'm here and I'm queer, so get used to it!
Ric Flair. The coolest mofo on earth.
You only please on your knees.
Smash the fascists!
There is a wall inside us all.

I heard applause and whistles as I washed my hands. The evening's next round of entertainment was about to begin. As I made my way over to our table the compère was spinning the barrel. She pulled a ball out and called the number on it in both German and English. As she read out the numbers of each drawn ball, corresponding digits on our strips of paper were diligently crossed or circled (or in the case of Caprice with her own personal felt tip pen the size of a microphone, stamped with a silk-gloved flourish). Eventually a man at a table at the back called out 'house', which was greeted with groans from many. He weaved through the tables and up to the stage to collect his prize. The trolley was then wheeled off and the lights on the stage went out. I could see movement on the stage but could not work out what the figures, blanketed in partial darkness, were doing.

Caprice said to us in hushed tones, 'Oh, this next act is creepy.'

'She is from Belgium,' Stella said.

'She's very good.'

'What is it?' K. asked.

'Just wait and see, dear.'

When the set up was complete the spotlight came on, focusing on the front of the stage as the compère returned.

'Now, ladies and gentlemen, we have the amazing Cecilia!'

The spotlight shifted. At the back of the stage was a rectangular box six feet in height. It had a black matt finish, stood vertically and was propped up against the far wall of the stage. As the compère went over to the box a sombre soundtrack started. She pulled the lid back to reveal yet another man in drag – although his make-up was applied in a less conventional fashion. The amazing Cecilia had his/her eyes closed. He/she was dressed head to toe in black – a black ankle length gown and a black choker. As the music built to its melancholy climax the eyes opened slowly to look out at the audience. The face was made grotesque by the makeup (a broad swathe of black above and below the eyes the most jarring). Caprice put a hand to her mouth and took in an audible breath, either in anxiety or in attempt to suppress a laugh. The crowd were utterly still.

Cecilia then spoke; the words slow, heavy and portentous:

'I am Cecilia, awoken from the dark night. I know the past and I see the future. Ask me a question and you will be answered truly.'

The compère turned to the audience.

'Come on, boys and girls. Any questions?'

A man stood up and asked, 'Who will win the Bundesliga?'

'Be serious now, pets.'

A woman then stood up, egged on by her friends.

'Will I be married?' she asked in a reedy voice.

'Not with thighs like that,' Caprice whispered.

'Unless he's myopic,' Stella added.

Cecilia blinked slowly before answering.

'Yes. But not until the autumn of your years.'

'Do you know who?' the woman asked.

'Someone you know already. That is all I will say.'

A short man with close-cropped dyed hair then raised his

arm. He stood, trying hard to suppress a smirk, and spoke with a Latin accent.

'I am opening a boutique soon. Will I be rich next year?'

Cecilia's eyes closed and opened again in slow motion. 'Look for material gain and you will find only dust. To have is not to be. I see a man at your shoulder. He has a message.'

'Is he cute?' the short man joked.

'He wears a brown flat cap and has a stoop.'

'Ohmigod! My grandfather?'

'Why does he have a stoop?' the compère asked him.

'He died of polio,' the man said breathlessly. 'Is he here? In Germany?'

'Life and the afterlife are one and the same. He wants me to tell you to look after yourself better. The drugs have to stop – or you will join him sooner that you should.'

The man looked shocked. He sat down without saying any more.

'Oh, spooky,' Stella said.

I had wanted to make a cynical comment to K. but something the man in the box had said stopped me. I saw, too, that she sat transfixed by his words.

'Next question,' said the compère.

K. stood up.

'Don't do it,' I said to her.

Caprice shushed me.

'Don't be a spoilsport. Let her ask.'

K. looked down at me. 'I want to know,' she said.

The compère shielded her eyes from the stage lights to make her out.

'Yes, dear, ask Cecilia your question.'

'What do you see in my future?' she asked.

Cecilia was silent for a while before answering in a mono-toned voice:

'Death follows you. From the Garden of Eden to the garden of ghosts. I see you, running between rows of black stones, the sun low, passing between them. A man follows you into the maze. Salvation comes from above.'

'How long do I have to live?' It was barely a whisper but Cecilia seemed to have heard her.

'Until dawn tomorrow.'

K. collapsed in her seat.

The compère rushed over to Cecilia and slapped her on the face. There was a delayed reaction before she put her hands up to her face and gave out a bleat of surprise.

'No more questions,' the compère hastily said. 'Thank you ladies and gentlemen. Thank you.'

Stella reached over the table. 'Oh, that awful fake! Don't take her seriously, my sweet,' she said.

Caprice proffered a glass. 'Here, drink some vodka.'

K. turned to me with a look on her face I hadn't seen before. 'Stay with me tonight,' she said.

I was sitting at the end of the bed. She was standing over me, stripping slowly. I watched as her clothes came off, one garment at a time.

Their apartment had the clutter and saccharin colour of a doll's house. Even the room K. was staying in, which was a spare bedroom, had a confectionary feel. We had been sitting in the living room sharing a bottle of dry white wine for most of the rest of the night. Stella and Caprice had gamely tried to lift the mood with Edith Piaf songs and other routines, but it had had little effect. The compre of the night had been with us, too, her large frame constantly shifting with discomfort in one of their antique chairs.

'We've had her before and she's been a riot,' she had said. 'She's had all sorts of visions. But she's never done that before.

She was too dark tonight.'

Caprice, who had been trying to fix a loose scarlet nail, had looked over at K..

'She's split up with that painter of hers recently. She was just cranky. That's all. Pay no heed to what she said.'

K. had been paying little attention to anything said then, though. She had nursed her glass of wine through most of the evening and had only occasionally smiled in gratefulness at the efforts of her flatmates. She was not smiling then.

'She said I had until dawn.'

'They don't know where you are,' I had said to her.

She hadn't listened.

'I knew they would come for me.'

At that precise moment the door bell had sounded. Everyone had jumped in their seats, but no one had moved to answer it.

'I'll get it,' I had said.

'Go with him, pet,' Stella had said to the compère, who had struggled out of the chair to follow me down the hall. The door did not have a spy glass. I had looked back at the hulking figure in sequins behind me before opening it. On the step had been a man wrapped in a thick peach-coloured cashmere sweater.

'Oh Franzi!' the compère had cried out in relief. 'Come in, come in. It's okay, we know him,' she had said to me before turning to the others who had been crowding the far end of the hall. 'It's just Franzi.'

The man at the door had pulled a face. 'Just? Charming,' he had said.

It had been not long after I had returned to the seat next to K. that she had downed her drink and had said to me: 'Let's go to my room.'

A clasp came off. Then a second earring. The skirt settled at her feet. I took my jacket off while watching her and noticed briefly that I still had the vial of painkillers in one pocket. I had forgotten. The Anarchist would be on the alcohol again tonight to dull the pain.

She needed solace, she needed to lose herself. I could see that. I was happy to oblige. But the moment I had often thought about, now it had arrived, was devoid of the elation and intensity I had imagined. As she stripped for me solemnly I could only sit there and watch. I felt strangely numb. My eyes fixed on hers as she undressed, but occasionally drifted down to take in the newly exposed flesh of a shoulder, the navel, a thigh, a breast. Part by part the geography of her was revealed to me and I explored with my eyes the ridges and contours, the clefts and curves. But it was more with a rising trepidation than anything else that I greeted our new level of intimacy. With the sound of her breathing and the increasing tempo of a pulsing heart in my ears came the echo of a distant warning. With every grave removal of an item of clothing, with every new unveiling, I felt the removal, brick by brick, of something else, something protective, that would expose us to a malignancy waiting beyond. I felt then that every new disclosure in her strip brought us closer to our doom.

It was not until she was completely naked that I reacted, taking her in my arms. I whispered to her hoarsely, 'Everything is going to be okay.'

She bit my shoulder then put her lips to one ear. 'Al youm, habibi, pleasure is a freedom song.'

9th November | 1945

A wonderful thing happened this morning. A mouse jumped on my mattress then ran off between some boxes. I did not scream, but initially it made me feel even more lonely than before. I decided to look for the mouse but there are so many places for them to hide it is impossible. I discovered a box full of Mother's old things which I think the mouse wanted me to find. It has really cheered me up. I put on the brown suede hat she wore to mass on Sundays. The feather was bent now and the hat slipped down over my ears. There was a compact with a mirror which made me sneeze when I dabbed too much on the cheek, which is silly because I have used powder before and there is so much dust up here I should be used to it by now. I could look like my mother in a few years. I have her face. Grandpa has said this, too. Then I found a gramophone record. It was Lilian Harvey singing "It only happens once". Mama's song! I am going to play the record. No one will hear. I am in an attic a long way from the street.

Grandpa appeared and shouted at me to turn off the record. He told me to slide a tea box over the hatch. It was very heavy but I managed it. Grandpa was very anxious and now I am scared.

I can hear them now. They are in the corridor below and Grandpa is shouting at them. Brave Grandpa! But they don't

understand him. Some are laughing, which sounds like
barking. I think of our Schnauzer that went missing soon after
we stopped going to the shops when the rationing ended. He
would protect us. They are poking at the hatch with rifles
but the tea box is keeping it from opening fully. Grandpa has
stopped shouting now.

They are still in the corridor, but they have stopped poking. I
can still hear them. Why don't they go away? Go away!

They are poking again.
   Please. Please go away.

05/11 | Don't say a prayer for me now

I awoke and experienced a brief moment of disorientation. I expected to see one bedroom and was instead presented with the pink hued walls and brightly painted furniture of another. Where was I? Then a body briefly stirred next to me and I remembered. I remembered everything. I remembered then, too, what is what like to wake up next to someone you really cared about. Whatever the size, whatever the number of layers on top of it, no bed is warm or comfortable enough without the lodestone of another's body beside you, the body of one you care about – at least at first, when the quality of sleep is of a tertiary concern. What a precious thing, a body. A body next to yours, helpless, vulnerable, lost in trusting slumber. The breathing faint, deep and regular – the gentle advance and retreat of the tides on sandy shores.

I hoped the morning hours dragged their feet, stretched on to prolong this feeling. In that moment I felt nothing could touch us, nothing could spoil these moments adrift together. Then a pang of discomfort hit me. I contemplated belatedly the possibility that I was projecting onto her an image that I wanted to see rather than what was actually there. What did I see? Was I guilty of the dissolving views of the male slideshow, seeing man's filtered image of womanhood, rather than absorbing her true nature; that paternalistic, chauvinistic habit of encoding rather than decoding femininity? I looked over at her. She was facing away from me, the duvet up to her shoulder imperceptibly rising and falling. An *Ausländer*. German for 'outsider', normally referring to migrants or foreigners in the country. *Ausländer* is what I felt then with her. A foreigner, an outsider, staring hopelessly at the divide, wondering how to get across. Then again, no matter how close we get to another person, no matter how close we feel, we are always on the outside. There is always a divide, a moat between us and the core of another, the place where the true self resides – with its insecurities, its bewilderments, its hurt. The place where the inner child hides, curled up in a foetal ball, refusing to come out into the light. With her the more she let me in, let me close, the more I felt that gap, that barrier between myself and her true nature. We are but a few inches apart (I could feel the glow of her body curled up under the sheets beside me), but it was as if we were separated by a gulf of white cotton, a wide stretch of ribbed and bunched bedspread. If I reached out to touch her it would be as if stretching out an arm over the lip of the Grand Canyon. Perhaps it is the distance that allures; the untameable, the unknowable or, in the case of her former lover from Beirut, the un-ownable. What was she to me? Moreover, what was I to her? We had talked about relationships before, but in more general terms. I remembered her line about voles: 'Only five per cent of mammals are monogamous. Us and voles and other foolish animals. There's a good reason why 95% of mammals don't stick to one partner.' For once, it seemed, she would prefer to go with the majority.

I dozed again for a while, but soon awoke with the feeling that something was lightly brushing my chest, like the fevered wings of a trapped moth. I opened my eyes and instead saw that she had wrapped herself around me as I lay on my back, her face resting on my upper body. She was obviously awake, rapidly blinking on my chest.

'That's nice,' I murmured. 'A butterfly kiss.'

She looked up at me, face slightly lost, as if she had been thinking deeply about something. The smile took a while to reach her lips. 'You like butterfly kisses?' she asked.

I lifted her chin. 'I do. But I like the real thing even more. Congratulations, by the way,' I said.

'What do you mean?'

'I mean, it's way past dawn and you are still alive.'

'Yes. Yes. She was wrong about the time.'

'Wrong, full stop. You don't still believe that so-called clairvoyant, do you?'

Her mouth tensed for a moment. As she thought she breathed through her nose, her nostrils dilating.

'She had never seen me before, yet she knew I was marked for death.'

'Don't be silly.'

'She saw that. She got the day wrong, that's all.'

'Then all you have to do is oversleep.'

'It is not funny.'

'I'm sorry. We English have a habit of using black humour in difficult situations.'

She returned to resting her head on my chest, eyes blinking.

'The look on her face. She saw my future. She saw it. She saw me die,' she said.

'First of all, she is a *he*. That's the first obvious deception. The second is that *he* is an acquaintance of your new flatmates. He probably overheard some gossip they let slip before the show. You're not going to die, not now and not here. I won't let you die.'

But she didn't hear me. She was somewhere else.

'I called my father yesterday. Little Anisha said there were men waiting for her outside her school. They had said they were friends of my father come to pick her up and she went with them.'

'What happened?'

'They took her home. They drove her home. Don't you see? They were threatening my family. My family! We will never be free of him.'

'Don't say that. Listen, I've been thinking. I'm considering going back to England for a while. Come with me. You can start again there.'

She looked up at me, her mascara patchy in places.

'And what happens when they follow me to England? What happens to my family.'

'Time will dull his fury. His anger will dim and he will forget you. You must disappear for a while. Off the radar. You must–'

'Have you heard of Hezbollah?' she asked.

'Of course.'

'He was a member of the Central Council before he became a businessman. The Hezbollah's roots run deep into my country. And beyond. There are many who are willing to die in their name. There are many equally willing to kill in their militia.'

'But it doesn't change the fact that–'

She stopped me. 'Could you kill someone? If they, if there was no alternative. Could you do it?' she asked.

'Kill?'

Her face was blank. 'Help end their life – if there was no alternative. For the sake of others. Could you?'

'Lose these thoughts. Now. No one is killing anyone and no-one is going to die.'

'People have already died because of me.'

'We don't know for sure. But we will know if we go to the police.'

'No.'

'We are withholding information that may be crucial.'

'No.'

'I'm not comfortable with this, K.. We can't stay silent forever.'

During my speech she had started shaking her head, gently at first then increasingly violently, until she burst out: 'No, no, no!' and started beating at my face and chest as best she could in her prone position. I tried to grab and restrain her pummelling arms, using soft words to soothe her, but she was getting ever more frantic and the screams were rising in pitch. She leapt off the bed and started throwing random items to hand at me. I climbed out on the other side of the bed, warding off a hairbrush, CDs and items of clothing. There was a loud knock on the door and an anxious voice called out. I opened it, realising belatedly that I was naked.

'What's going on?' Stella asked, before retreating behind the door as one of my shoes hit. The head reappeared and turned accusing eyes on me. 'What have you done?'

'Get out. Get out!' K. screamed.

'Me?' Stella asked her.

K. pointed an egg-shell blue vase at me.

'No, you! Get out!'

I stared at her, not being able to find the words. She raised her arm.

'Darling, not the china,' Stella's normally soft feminine voice was forgotten briefly in alarm and a shocking deep baritone sounded instead. K.'s arm went back. A commanding tenor stopped her in mid-toss. 'Nein! Not the vase!' Stella's feminine voice returned as she turned back to me. 'I think you'd better go.'

I looked at the girl on the other side of the bed. Her chest lifted with every shallow breath, her face full of paused fury. Words were useless now. I pulled my clothes off the back of a chair and quickly dressed as she stood and watched, clutching the vase tightly.

Could you kill? The other lovers, had she asked the same of them? Some of them would do it without hesitation, I was sure of that. They did not have to be cajoled to step through the breach for her.

As I made my way to the apartment door de-wigged heads appeared and shook in disapproval at the perceived betrayal of their trust. Clucking voices in German followed me out and the apartment's door slammed in my back.

It was a long ride to Prenzlauer Berg. I had to make several changes and at Friedrichstrasse there was an uncharacteristic delay that left me impatiently pacing the length of the platform. I stopped at one end, stood on the lip and stared into the gaping hole of the tunnel, willing a train to arrive. I thought about texting something to her but decided against it. The Black Dog was at my heel. My clothes stank of cigarettes and my head was full of conflicting thoughts; unspoken words left dangling on dry lips. I was thirsty and hungry – I felt generally empty. To occupy my mind I thought of buying some Schrippen, freshly baked white rolls, on the way back. I would buy them from the small bakery run by a friendly Turkish girl. I thought about the fried egg and ham and melted grated cheese and Sambal chilli sauce I would fill it with. Hang it, I would buy a slice of her New York cheesecake for afters, too.

A young couple were fooling about on the platform's edge close by. He had a hardback book in his hand and she wanted to look at it. He would not let her and a playful tug of war ensued that soon turned into a clinch and a deep French kiss. *Get a room.* I turned away to smother curmudgeonly thoughts.

But they were on the other side as well. The rectangular mirror at the platform's end showed most of its length, there so the driver could see from his cabin if everyone was on board. I saw the bottom half of the two lovers entwined in the mirror. He had one arm around her waist, the other with the book down at his side. The reflection reversed the title: FLOWNEPPETS. I looked at it for a second and then something inside my head did the same thing to a snagged quark of information.

Bingo.

I fumbled for my mobile phone. I dialled her number. She was not answering, surprise, surprise. I texted her:

I know you're angry but call me. I know who your flash mob author is.

I shook my head and managed a rueful smile. *Well, well.* At that moment the train arrived. I got in, allowing the love birds on first. I sat down eager for the train to leave but no door alarm sounded. It was being held at the station for some reason. Most unusual. My phone rang. *Well, well.* I pulled it out of my coat pocket. It was not her.

'Sassenach!'

'What's up?'

'Where have you been, you naughty Englishman?'

'I went to that cabaret show I told you about. Remember?'

'Yes, and then?'

'We went back to the owner's for drinks?'

'And then?' A pause. 'And theeeeeeen?'

'I stayed over.'

'I knew you were the tranny-loving type.'

'Whoever said the German's have no sense of humour was obviously from Austria.'

'We do have a sense of humour, my friend. It's just not your little island's sense of humour. Anyway, if you don't want to tell me if you got jiggy with the singer, that's fine. Just tell me you've got my bloody pills!'

I patted a coat pocket.

'Your mouth still hurts?'

'Yeah 'cos you haven't given me the bloody pills! Christ, it's like you're my dealer. I'm waiting for my man. I knew I shouldn't have asked you to get them for me.'

I patted another coat pocket. 'Alright, keep your shaggy hair on,' I said.

'When are you coming back, Englishman? I want my pills.'

I searched an inside pocket.

'Give me half an hour, then you will get your drugs.'

'Hurry up, or I hit your whiskey again to numb the ache.'

I hung up and searched every pocket. Twice. *Shit*. I must have left it at the apartment. I had to go back. This was going to be awkward. Either way, someone would be less than pleased to see me. I thought about another text and soon dismissed it and jumped out of the still stationary train to head back the way I had come.

It took a while for the door to open, but eventually it did. Stella's mouth hardened when she saw who it was.

'What do *you* want?'

'I'm not here to cause trouble, I promise. I left some pills and–'

'What *kind* of pills?'

'Nothing serious, just some painkillers. They are for a friend. He needs them. I left them in the bedroom.'

'Wait here. She's gone back to bed.'

She left the door ajar and I listened as Stella tapped on the bedroom door.

'Darling? Sweet. Are you awake? Can I come in? Darling? She's not answering.'

'I need them, I'm sorry.'

She knocked again, louder this time.

'Darling, hallo. Hallo? Sweetie?'

Caprice and the compère appeared out of another room, wrapped in matching kimonos.

'What is it? What's going on?' Caprice asked.

'K. is not answering and the door's locked.'

'I think my pills are there,' I said to them.

'What exactly were your pills?' Stella asked.

'Painkillers. Oh shit.'

'You don't think…?'

Stella's baritone voice came back. 'Open this door now, or we will have to break it!' she shouted.

No response.

'Alright, enough monkeying around,' I said. 'Step back.' I barged the door. And again. It refused to budge.

'Step back,' the compère said. 'Step back! Ein, zwei, drei!'

She took a run up and shoulder charged the door. Her larger frame did the trick and the lock gave way with the sound of splintering wood. K. was lying utterly still on the bed in her undergarments, the disturbance unmoving her. Her face was calm, ashen. On the sideboard was the vial of pills. The cap was off.

'She's taken the pills,' I said.

'Oh Scheisse! How many?'

'I don't know, but it looks like a lot.'

'It hasn't been long,' Stella said. She slapped her face, bellowing, 'Wake up. Wake up!'

'Carry her into the bathroom,' the compère said. 'Stick her under a cold shower. We have to wake her up.'

'Wait. She's stirring.'

The painted eyelids flickered then slowly rose – heavy doors to an ancient vault.

'Darling,' Stella said. 'Can you hear me?'

K. groaned.

'How many pills did you take? Answer me.'

The answer came in the form of a projectile of vomit, straight up into Stella's face.

How can any creature on this planet still look appealing while ejecting stomach bile and making pitiful retching sounds? How? It was just as well she no longer had long hair, it would have made a rather sticky impediment as she kneeled over the toilet. Tears of effort from her scrunched up eyes had collected on the tips of her lashes. Red blotches were blooming on her tensed neck.

She tried to force words out between the heaves. They sounded like, 'I'm sor. I wa… my fam…'

I rubbed her back.

'It's okay. It's okay. Just get it all out.'

When her body had ceased in its efforts to expel the toxins I said, 'I have something that might cheer you up.'

She looked at me over the toilet bowl, blinking back the tears, wiping away a stray drip of spittle from her chin.

'I doubt that.'

'I got some news. I know who your flash mob author is, and why the author has gone quiet.'

My love,

I am writing this in prison. A military prison I estimate to be one and a half hour's drive from Berlin. I asked for a pencil and a piece of paper. My guard eventually gave me some sheets and a pencil the length of your pinkie finger. I suppose they thought I was going to write a confession. I write very small and hope it fits. The slot often slides back and a pair of eyes watches me as I scratch out this letter to you. Watching the watchers. I know for a fact that someone watches them, too. I had asked for the paper outside in the corridor as I was escorted by the guard to my cell. He had hissed to me, "Shut up, traitor." A red light at the end of the corridor had come

175

on and he had shoved me into the wall. "Face the wall. Do not turn your head. Say nothing." Two sets of footsteps went past, another guard and his prisoner, no doubt. I wondered who it was and what they had done. A cell door clanged and I was marched on to my cell, the red light at the end of the corridor was off. A green bulb beside it was then lit. The smell of linoleum in the corridor made me think of my parents. The bare walls of my cell make me think of you.

I was with Matze, patrolling by the stadium. It was late evening. I wanted to talk about what was happening in Hungary and Czechoslovakia. He wanted to talk about his conquests. He was in the middle of a ribald account of one of his latest lays. He had chatted her up at a queue for the bakery, promising the inside track to some black market goods. We were at a point equidistant from two towers. Matze had stopped to urinate on the column track. He was waving an arc of urine back and forth as he boasted, the dwindling stream shaking as he convulsed with laughter at his own joke. I turned away to look back the way we had come and that is when I saw them in the glare of magnesium floodlights. Two young men in faded denim running across the strip at either end of a ladder approximately three metres in length. They had just finished negotiating the signal fence and were sprinting as best they could for the border wall. Matze saw them too, then. He pissed himself as he frantically tried to finish and do himself up with the rifle slipping off his shoulder, shouting, "Fuck, fuck!" Instinctively I cried "Halt!" I was just as shocked as he was to see them. Escapees. In the flesh! "Halt!" I cried again. "Halt, or we will open fire!" They, of course, did not heed my challenge. Why had they not waited until we were further up the track? I levelled my rifle. "Halt!" They were ten metres from the Wall now. "Halt!" "Shoot the bastards," Matze shouted. "What are you waiting for?" I didn't shoot. Instead I

176

lowered my weapon and raced off towards them, across the carefully raked sand, Matze cursing behind me. They reached the Wall. I stopped. I would not get there in time. Multiples of voices screamed in my head; different commands, including Matze's. He was beside me now. His rifle came up. The ladder was being raised. One face turned back towards us, eyes wide in panic. Matze angled his head to rest his chin on the rifle and closed one eye to train his sights on them. The finger on the trigger squeezed. He didn't see the butt of my rifle.

I looked over to the Wall. One of them scaled the ladder and threw a blanket over the anti-climb pipe. The other climbed up behind him until they were both at the top. Their bodies were stiff, no doubt expecting the blow of a bullet at any second. The first, with the aid of his companion, clambered over the anti-climb pipe and disappeared. The second, gripping the now taut blanket, soon followed, leaving the ladder propped against the Wall. I looked down at Matze spitting blood at my feet. I kicked his rifle away, then looked back at the ladder. "You crazy fuck!" he screamed. "What have you done?" Just then a patrol vehicle raced past a watchtower and headed down the column track in our direction. My mind froze. I don't know why but I could not move. The Wall was there to be scaled. It was at my mercy. It was my chance. You were beyond that wall. But my legs failed me then. My head failed me. I could not force myself forward. Matze had stopped cursing and was now laughing. It was either the drink or the look on my face. He rolled in the sand until his laughs were drowned out by the vehicle's engine.

It is over for me now. I imagine your life. Where in the world are you right now? Are you thinking of me? How long would you wait for me? Chased every day by rich West Germans – pestering you with unimaginable gifts, offering unlimited wealth and security. Could I fault you for giving in

177

to such offers? You *may* have done it already. You *may* be carrying a *new* passport with a *new* surname and carrying a growing child in your belly. If you are, then fuck you!

I'm sorry. I cannot take it being without you anymore. It is over. My hand is trembling as I write this now. What is the point of writing this? It will not make it past these walls, let alone reach you. All those letters at home. No doubt discovered. Evidence. All those words. All for nothing.

My life is over. I will time the seconds between the monitoring slot going back and then

It seems I can't stop writing, even though I know the only people who will read this will be my gaolers – and I have no words for them. They are prisoners as much as I am.

Goodbye, my love. I hope you are happy.

08/11 | Dig for victory

She was late. They would already be gathering at the site. No matter. They knew basically what needed to be done. Mercifully, it was a glorious day. I waited for her at the station and enjoyed the midday sun on my face.

We live in the past – even the light we live by is old.

I looked around and tried to imagine what life was like on this spot twenty years ago. Then sixty years ago. How things had changed. The Anarchist – through swollen jaw – had expounded on the notion of freedom over a glass of Bushmills at lunch. Freedom of expression, freedom of movement, freedom of anonymity. There are different levels of freedom, he had said. And some impressions of freedom were illusory. Only a few cities could genuinely claim to offer complete freedom to its citizens. Berlin, he said, was one of those, citing examples: demonstration without hindrance; minimal police presence; minimal CCTV intrusion. I started to look around the street for closed circuit cameras. I found none of those invasive eyes that we in the UK accepted on our streets, or were simply indifferent to now. I thought of another aspect to city life that we begrudgingly accepted – young drunks on our streets after dark, collapsing in shop fronts, barking into inverted traffic cones, looking for fights to compliment their night. Berlin is far from being free of drunkenness and violence, but you rarely saw at taxi stands or outside kebab shops what you would sadly see in most English towns or city centres at night. Pissed males out to provide a violent compliment to their revelry, out to reaffirm their masculinity, to bury sexual frustration or negate the weight of general failure; to give vent to inarticulate fury at the banality of their lives; to forget tomorrow's soul-sapping shift at that industrial park or chain store.

'Come friendly bombs, rain on Slough.'

An attractive woman went by, well-dressed, the street her catwalk. She was aware of my stare but did not meet it, and instead looked the other way, taking notice of a café display indicating a coffee and doughnut discount. Women on Berlin streets often throw up a wall of self-protection – they are aware of the looks, the covetous glances, the flirtatious games men play for self-validation, but they seldom play along, lest they give the wrong impression.

Perhaps a woman will return a glance here and there if an equally attractive male catches her eye – but mostly the wall, the *mauer,* is up, insulating her from the one-track thoughts of the opposite sex.

'Sorry I'm late. Have you been waiting long?'

She had managed to make her way over to me without me noticing. How does she do that? I would not have made a good *Stasi* agent, that's for sure. I told her I hadn't been there long, looking at the halo of sunlight over her head that had taken eight minutes to reach us.

'I was a little anxious taking the metro. I kept jumping off and on again at the last second.'

'You didn't see anyone follow you?'

'No, although I saw suspicious faces everywhere I looked. It's making me crazy.'

'Let's go,' I said. 'The others will be there waiting.'

We talked as we walked quickly to the site. We talked about

other events Nasus had organised and whom K. had attended. Hugging the conspiracy theorists who loitered at the station we had met at; helping short-staffed workers at a soup kitchen for the homeless; a 'Bonfire of the Vanities' night where symbolic items of 'aesthetic fascism' had been incinerated. All very worthy. She was a thoughtful cookie, no question. And a playful one, too. Time to reap a little of what she had sown electronically.

I caught K. looking briefly in a passing shop front at her reflection as we walked. She obviously was not sure about her new look. I remembered reading that if you travelled at the speed of light and, for some reason, had a mirror with you and looked into it you would not see your own reflection. There would be nothing there. You would be turned into a space vampire by the immutable laws of physics.

'This is a wonderful idea,' she said to me absently patting her hair. 'She will love it, I'm sure.'

'I hope it helps.'

'It will. I'm sure of it.'

There was quite a crowd that greeted us. Most of the usual suspects that K. had managed to contact were there, and most were carrying a variety of gardening implements. They had collected on a vacant lot on a street corner that was scheduled for development. It was a cheese wedge patch of weeds and brambles and littered with household rubbish, including a tattered sofa. A half-burnt pallet sat in the remains of a small fire in the centre.

Stella and Caprice were there, conservatively dressed in dungarees, their bewigged heads wrapped in silk scarves. When they saw us they raised garden tools in a revolutionary salute. 'Guerrilla gardeners at the ready!' they cried.

We set about our beautification, our transformation of the derelict space. Once it was denuded of weeds and rubbish the real job could begin. Referring occasionally to a schematic one of the more creative members had drawn up, the group set about digging and planting. A van-load of unwanted plants and flowers mostly acquired at a flea market arrived. As we planted we were serenaded with uplifting music by one of the buskers from Alexanderplatz. A few children lingered nearby on the corner with their parents looking on intently.

Towards the end of the afternoon the space took shape. We had dug out a large circular patch of earth into which we planted evenly spaced rows of vegetables and plants, all angled to converge in the centre, where carefully arranged carnations and other flowers had been planted. Two volunteers had opened a few bags of shingle and were going around the circumference of our cultivated space, scattering the stones liberally to make a path. It was almost done.

When seen from a vantage point the efforts of the group would reveal a wheel-shaped allotment with lines of vegetables, plants and bamboo supports for spokes; and at its core, a riot of colour.

'It's magical,' K. said, a spot of physical work having lifted the tension from her shoulders. 'It's her wheel.'

'It's a chakra,' a volunteer overhearing said. 'A Buddhist symbol – Life in movement. Death in stagnation.'

I looked over at the apartment building directly across the street facing the site and counted the floors. I scanned the windows on the fifth floor where I had been told her bedroom was. It had been difficult to get the information, which was understandable considering the sensitivity of the job her father did, but I had a man on the inside. And then I saw a face peering out from the apartment window. A woman's face, in her fifties, perhaps. She was talking to someone in the room with her… *There!* Only the top of the head could be seen, just above the windowsill. A hairless head. The eyes betrayed an unseen smile – a half-exposed face full of delight and incredulity.

Yes, this is for you. Get well soon, Susan. There are people out in the ether that need you.

Lost weekend | Lyle

Where the fuck did I leave my bike?

Lyle walked up the street in the direction he thought he'd left it. His steps were steady but cautious, as if he was walking on a rope bridge that threatened to give way at any second. One hand turned the keys to his bike lock around their metal hoop like an Arab's prayer beads.

Laughter drew his attention from the scrutiny of the cobbled street to the side of the canal where he recognised the same group of Italians that had been with them in the coffee shop. They were laughing and pointing at something in the canal. Lyle was aware their giggling fit could have been triggered by even the most innocuous sights so he paid little heed. A dope high did that to you, he knew. Sometimes it produced in him a juvenile convulsion that threatened never to leave; the more he wanted to stop laughing the greater the compulsion to laugh. Lyle realised they were standing at the spot where he had left his bike and walked over. As he approached he heard the sound of splashing and a muted voice in distress over the Italian guffaws. Lyle looked over the edge of the street down into the canal and saw what they were laughing at: someone was in the water.

A blood-smeared face fixed with a look of panic was spinning around in the greenish soup. Propelled by bare wind-milling arms the man gave little whelps as he struggled to keep his head above the oil smeared-surface, snatching air through puckered lips like a manic fish. Near him, but being pushed away by his thrashing, was a bobbing black dildo. The Italians were now in hysterics. It was clear that the man could not swim and, soon enough, he lost his battle to keep his head above the surface, not before letting out a high-pitched cry for help.

Jason?

After a moment's hesitation, Lyle tried to pull his windbreaker over his head, but only succeeded in pitching into the water headfirst sooner than he intended.

09/11 | Der Himmel über Berlin

That morning she had left the apartment while I was still asleep. The day had passed with faltering attempts to find work, any kind of work, to fill the ensuing days and help re-focus. Hell, if George Orwell could work as a *plongeur* in Paris, I thought, then I could not turn my nose up at any form of employment.

It was not until late afternoon that I heard from her.

'I have been followed all day,' she said on the phone.

'Are you sure? By whom? What did they look like?'

'Like my shadow.'

'Where are you?'

'Meet me. I have to tell you something.'

'Where?'

'I'm going to send you a text.'

'A text?' I asked.

She'd hung up. Not long after an SMS from her came through detailing where and when to meet.

The Tiergarten: a cultivated carpet of nature that rolled out westward from the Brandenburg Gate. There are many small monuments dotted throughout, but the one we had agreed to meet at was one of the closest to the city's biggest tourist draw. When I finally found it in a wedge of open green, I was not surprised to find that she was not there waiting for me. At least it gave me time to compose my thoughts and work out what I was going to say to her if she did turn up.

Although cold, it was not a bad day to be loitering in the park. There were a few other people about, but none looked suspicious – just lovers and dog walkers idling along the path dotted with lampposts with glass bulbs shaped like snowdrops with bent stalks, as if weighed down by morning dew. The three-sided monument was a dedication to some of the classical world's greatest composers: Beethoven, Haydn and Mozart. At the top three gold leaf clad cherubs held aloft a laurel leaf. On each side, along with the likeness of a composer, was a liver bird or a swan with wings outstretched and a collection of golden instruments, plus dramatic faces set in rictuses of joy and despair.

A man on a nearby bench called out. His Dalmation, who had been zig-zagging across the grass, was now making a beeline for an Alsation idling by the waters of a nearby pond examining the unconcerned ducks gliding through the reeds at its fringes. My mobile vibrated in my pocket and I fished it out.

'Hello?'

'Who do you like best?'

'Sorry?'

'Which composer?'

I looked around for her. 'Where are you?'

'Which composer?'

Some things will never change, I thought. 'Hard to choose. Mozart, I suppose,' I said.

'They all look so moody, so serious, don't they? Turn a little bit to your right.'

I did and faced the direction of an ugly squat stone structure with a sloping corrugated roof. It looked like a half-finished bunker with its one exposed side. I saw a face peering out at me through the gap between roof and wall. The eyes smiled briefly out at me. I hung up and made my way over to her. She stood inside hugging herself as if warding off the cold. The inside walls were unsurprisingly covered in graffiti; the low roof, which was only a few feet above her head, was set on exposed slanting wooden beams. She was looking out onto the stretch of water beside the bunker, the late afternoon sun in her face.

'I used to take little Anisha to the park to feed the birds. I would help break up the pita bread for her. But she always wanted to do it herself and would not break up the bread into small enough pieces.' She smiled. 'She used to throw these bits of pita bread at them making them scatter in panic.'

'You spoke to your family recently?'

'Yes.'

'Are they all right?'

'They are safe.'

I looked around. 'No one followed you here?'

'I don't think so. You?'

'I didn't notice anything.'

She said, 'I have been thinking about what you said. You're right. For the families of the others we must go to the police. But I want you to go. Tell them about the times you met these men. Tell them what you know. But I can't go.'

'How do I explain my connection to them? It's for your protection, you know.'

'You can tell them about me and what you know, but say you haven't seen me again.'

At that moment the Alsation came up to us, having skirted the pond to trail the ducks. His owner was following him round. I looked at the dog snuffling in the dirt at our feet. 'Let's walk,' I said.

We walked along a path that took us through the last stretch of trees at the park's edge. The sudden cry of a blackbird sounded, warning of our approach; its mate skipped away across the blanket of dead leaves. She looked up. A solitary white balloon was snagged in a tree's upper branch, its pitted matt surface indicating a slow death of deflation.

'I got some news today. Something from home. I don't know what it means—'

'What? What is it?'

'Last week a member of Hezbollah's Central Council was shot. He died in hospital yesterday.'

'And?'

'He was my ex-lover.'

'*The* ex-lover?'

'Yes.'

'Then it's over. Isn't it?'

'God willing, yes.'

I kissed her then. She held on to me tightly for a while before we drew apart. She plucked one of her hairs off my collar.

'I was thinking about what you said. About starting—'

Her eyes drifted over my shoulder and the warmth left her face.

'What is it?'

'My shadow.'

I looked round and saw a man in a long black coat standing a little way off the path. He was perfectly still, watching us, unconcerned of his discovery.

'Let's finish this,' I said, and started to walk over to him. She stopped me, tugging on my arm.

'No. He has seen us. He won't hesitate now.'

The man was some distance away but I could see his crooked smile which was slowly getting broader. He started walking towards us, one hand tucked firmly into a coat pocket.

She tugged at me. 'We have to leave. Now!'

We turned and swiftly walked toward the park's edge. We were on a broad circular patch of grass then, populated with modern sculptures. I could see cars and coaches through the last straggle of trees. Safety would come with mixing with other people. I looked around. He had picked up his pace to close the gap between us before we left the park.

'It might be best to start running.'

We hit tarmac. A busy road greeted us, traffic heading up and past the Brandenburg Gate to our left. Across the road, the maze of stones of the Holocaust Memorial. We ran across, making a coach slam on its brakes. It was not as busy as I had hoped. Pedestrians were light in number and there were only a few lingering tourists about, taking photographs of the site. One male tourist, in a brightly coloured ski jacket, was even balancing theatrically on a stone for his laughing girlfriend to photograph, seemingly oblivious to its significance.

I looked around. He was on the other side of the road, waiting for a space in the traffic to cross.

'Let's go in,' I said.

The stones were a uniform grey, irregularly sized and set on an undulating surface of small similarly coloured tiles – the floor a rippling wave of paving. The monoliths were like a flotilla of containers lost off the side of a cargo ship after a storm and drifting in an orderly mass on the dark distemper of the sea. We ran between them, the stones growing in height to swallow us.

'Stop here,' I said.

We leaned against a stone block, catching our breath, our backs to the way we had come. The stones around us had patches of darker grey, moisture that had yet to dry from the earlier downpour. I looked round the corner down the straight gap to the memorial's edge. I could not see him.

Suddenly, to my left a figure passed by. It was an Asian man with a camera looking for a killer angle, waiting for the sun to come back. It did, the clouds passed and it shone over the tops of the trees of the park and down between the stones. I saw him then. He passed between the stones down the gap I had been looking, from left to right.

'Come on.'

I took her further back, weaving this way and that, left then right, then left again. We stopped. I looked around the edge of the stone block. The sun was briefly extinguished by another passing cloud but soon returned. I felt her grip my arm with sudden intensity. I turned back. He was behind us, a gun out, a silencer screwed on to its muzzle. She said something to him in Arabic. He looked at her and that grimace came back, creasing his face, and with it a gleam of triumph in his eyes. Just then a shadow passed over us. He looked up to see someone standing above. He raised his gun and fired two rapid shots, the sound like someone spitting out melon seeds. A figure dropped to the floor, twitching. It was the tourist in the ski jacket.

'Achtung!'

A security guard was heading down between the stones towards us. The Turk turned and the guard stopped, noticing the gun. Without thinking I leapt on his back, the force relinquishing his grip on the pistol, sending it clattering across the tiles. I quickly applied a half-nelson, wrapping my hands up and around the back of his neck. He was immensely strong, throwing us back against a stone block, winding me. He tried a reverse head butt, but I had expected it and jerked my head away in time. We struggled on the floor. I was fast losing my grip when the security guard fell on us. Then another guard appeared on the scene and joined the melee. The combined weight turned the tide in our favour. The Turk's curses and fury eventually subsided and was replaced with maniacal laughter. One of the guards was shouting instructions down a walkie-talkie as the Turk relaxed.

'Okay, okay,' the man said.

I released my grip slowly and got to my feet. The guards turned him over and lifted him up, pinning his arms behind him. He locked eyes with me. That awful smile came back.

'You think you know her, Englishman? You think she is yours?' he said.

'Who are you?'

He hadn't finished. 'You know nothing about her. You are nothing to her. Nothing! You do not know her like I do.'

'Maybe.'

'You don't know what you have done, my friend. She is-'

He looked behind me, eyes scanning, his face losing its smug expression. I thought it was a trick and warily glanced around.

She was gone.

9th November | 1945

I hope this can be read at a later date. My handwriting is so squiggly, but I have to write this now. I am so excited I don't know what to do except try and write something.

The soldiers went away after their captain told them to. After a while Grandpa called up to me to move the chest and he came up the steps. I laughed when I saw him because he did not have his teeth in. Grandpa said they had broken his false teeth and said a rude word and told me not to laugh but I couldn't help it. He looked so funny without them. We laughed together for a while then Grandpa told me to be serious. He had decided that we should leave the city at once and he had asked Herrn Ziss, the watchmaker, if we could use his pushcart. Grandpa made me swear I would keep still when I was in the pushcart and not say a word. I was so excited to be going outside but I swore it, even though I was fed up with always hiding. Grandpa then made me put on many layers of old baggy clothes that smelt and took me down from the attic. I did not get to see the apartment as we went down to the front door, and I so desperately wanted to see inside.

The light was so bright outside! The eyes stung for a while. Big purple blotches bloomed in my lids when I blinked. The small cart was there, heaped with more old clothes. I climbed under them and then Grandpa and Herrn Ziss pushed me slowly up the road. After a while I couldn't resist a peek and I saw only little bits through the clothes, but I did see Mrs Paulaner's delicatessen, which was smashed and empty, and the cobblers, which was black. The buildings looked like they were made of leaves. A big wind had come and blown them everywhere. Sometimes the cart stopped and I could hear soldiers arguing with Grandpa and Herrn Ziss and I was scared. But the cart would move on and I could hear Grandpa and Herrn Ziss wheeze with the effort of pushing. After what seemed like a very long time they pulled the clothes off and we were on the edge of the city. A tractor was there, pulling another cart. This one was big with lots of people on it. Some children, too. Grandpa and I hugged Herrn Ziss goodbye and we climbed onto the tractor, which is now pulling us into the countryside.

Grandpa has just tried to do a bad thing. He has kept the medal my father won fighting in Russia. It has a red, white and black ribbon and is silver with a cross on it. I didn't know he still had it. He was going to throw it away into the passing trees. I grabbed his arm and shouted to him not to do it. I said to him it is all we have left of Papa. Grandpa listened to me, and after looking at it for a long time put it away again.

The sun is warm on my face and the wind moves my hair. It feels amazing! I am terribly hungry but still happy. I want to hear birds but the tractor is loud. I want Grandpa to whistle but he looks tired and is thinking. Perhaps he is thinking about Grandma or Mother or Father. Grandpa has butterflies, too.

I know, one day, my time in the attic will become a butterfly. But it will be one butterfly I won't try to catch.

10/11 | Echoes

The rain had just forced me to retreat from my bedroom balcony so I heard the knock at the apartment door. It was foolish but my heart started to race. I looked through the spy hole. It was Spiderman. He had tidied himself up and looked sober, but nothing could mask the ravaged face. I opened the door. In one hand, afflicted with a slight tremor, was a manila envelope stuffed with paper.

'I am sorry about the other day. I don't remember much about it – apart from the kindness of an English neighbour.'

'It was no trouble at all. I am glad to see you are better.'

'I am not better. But my mind is clearer. You saw me at a bad time. I was struggling to deal with the approach of an anniversary.' He looked at me intently. 'Is this a good time?'

'It's fine. Please come in.'

We sat at the kitchen table. I didn't have time to remove the nearly empty bottle of whiskey that stood to one side. He regarded it in a manner that suggested I had casually left a loaded gun out.

'Would you like a drink… of tea?'

'Danke. I hear you are a writer.'

'Well… I write. Occasionally.'

He tapped the manila envelope in front of him. 'I have brought these for you. I think you will appreciate them.'

'What is it?'

'It is a collection of voices. From the past. I will explain briefly if you don't mind: After I was fired from my professorship at Humboldt University, I struggled to find another placement. Who wants to employ an alcoholic? So I decided to try other means of employment, and eventually I got a job at the depot next door. I liked it. It made a welcome shift from the mental to the physical. I could just switch off.

As you can imagine, a lot of junk is left there. All sorts of unwanted waste from people's lives. One day I discovered some letters that had spilt out of a box. I took them home and read them. They gave me great... what is the word in English...?'

'Solace?'

'Yes, perhaps that is the word. After that, I would search through the discarded junk each day and collect all the personal papers I found. Mostly what I found was uninteresting, but that first discovery kept me looking. And sometimes my efforts were rewarded by other discoveries.'

'But why are you giving these to me?'

'I am going to Switzerland and I won't be coming back. I have no family. No one to pass them on to. And before last week I did not know a writer. Perhaps, if you wish, you can do something worthwhile with them.'

'But why don't you just take them to Switzerland with you?'

He chuckled, tapping the envelope. 'Because I am going to end my life in Switzerland. The alcohol is taking too long to kill me, so I have decided to bring the curtain down at a clinic there. My Eva is waiting for me. Have you been to Switzerland?'

'No.'

'Pretty. Always a neutral country. Jewish gold. Euthanasia.'

'That's why you are going.'

'Yes. I set the time and the date. I decide my destiny. How often can we say that? I wanted it to be November the ninth, the day my dear Eva died, but I cannot wait another year.'

'You should try and get them published yourself.'

He waved my words away. 'All too late. How long would I have to wait until some fish decides to bite? No, I cannot wait. There are too many people in this world as it is. I want to end my life on my terms. I chose not to rot away day by day. It is enough!'

'But… I can't read German.'

'I have translated them for you. The ones I love the most.'

I looked through the typed sheets. Most were begrimed by unknown foodstuffs and marked with red rings from wine glasses filled by an unsteady hand.

'You must excuse my written English,' he said. 'It is poor – and I may not do these voices justice – but you can read them and decide what to do.'

'There's so much here,' I said.

'This is just a small fraction. Most of what I have is nothing. These are a few of the diamonds in the coal dust. Do with them what you wish.'

'I don't know what to say.'

'Say, "Yes, I will take them!"' He reached across the table to take my hand. 'It is yours now. I have no use for them anymore. These voices deserve to be kept alive. But I am sick of the sound of my voice. For me, it is time for silence.'

November 9 | 1989

My love,

Something is happening. There are tooting of horns outside and shouting, but it's not some great accident. People rarely sound their horns without serious provocation, so it must be something BIG. Something momentous has happened. The people sound happy. I tried to climb the wall to reach the window but it is too high. I cannot make out what they are saying but there are many people in the streets now. What is going on? The guards are talking a great deal, but their words are muffled behind the cell door and they won't respond to my questions. It is so frustrating! I imagine having the strength of one hundred men and smashing down these walls, breaking through to freedom and your arms.

What a joyous thing that would be. Imagine if a mind could do that. Shatter walls. Love can, I suppose. My love for you stayed my hand when I thought of ending it all. Love conquers all!

Right now, millions of beating hearts in this country, like picks, are chipping away at the Wall. And eventually the Wall will give.

11/11 | These foolish things

I was woken by a deep resonant sound that came in regular waves, accompanied by a tremor that made the room shake. It was not thunder or a minor earthquake but the departing rubbish trucks from the waste depot next door. The ambassadors of morning. A procession of over twenty vehicles, one after the other, rumbling over the cobbled streets outside. It was six a.m.

I looked over and in the weak light afforded by the drawn curtains that hung from ceiling to floor saw the indentations of a head in the pillow next to me. There was single short stand of her hair left there. The morning after digging out the garden for Nitram/Susan, I had been woken by the same trucks and had seen the same strand. That time, though, the bed was still warm from her recent presence. The curtains had been partially drawn to reveal a slice of her sitting on a chair on the balcony outside smoking. She had had my coat on, and was bent slightly forward, her bare legs crossed, her top leg twitching as she exhaled smoke. She had rubbed her nose, picked at a green nail then drawn in another lungful of smoke. I had watched her gazing out in silent contemplation for a while and had thought about getting up and going over to her. Instead I had drifted off. When I had awoken an hour later both balcony and bed had been empty.

I moved across and rested on the other pillow. A subtle

scent of perfume lingered there. I breathed in through my nose. Outside a dog barked at the departing lorries.

A wolf of the steppes will occasionally, very rarely, happen upon another wolf. They will approach warily, circle, bare their fangs briefly, check each other's scent and, if of the opposite sex, couple for a while before moving on.

They might turn briefly at the crest of a hill to regard the other before disappearing out of sight. Instinct will always prevail, however. Later, they may encounter a scent of the other somewhere else; a marked spot of territorial claim – a fallen tree trunk, a boulder with moss covered on one side, perhaps – and through that scent the ghost of their encounter will linger. But in time that scent will fade.

The Anarchist was enjoying his morning black coffee at the kitchen table reading his broadsheet. There was enough in the pot for me so I joined him.

'Hey, you are in the news, man,' he said, tapping the paper. 'At least, the incident at the Jewish memorial is in the news. Do you want me to read it to you?'

'I'd rather you didn't.'

'Didn't take you long to get in the news, did it? Says here the man with the gun was a Syrian living in Berlin. Private detective. Probably paid to track her down. Looks like he got a bit carried away with his job. Don't say I didn't warn you about her.'

'I won't.'

'Cranky bear! Drink some coffee.'

I reached for the Bushmills. 'Think I might have an Irish this morning.'

'Jesus, that bad? You got a toothache, too?'

'Something like that.'

I felt eyes examine me over the top of the paper as I poured a liberal amount into the coffee.

'She got you bad. Still haven't heard from her?' he said.

I took a sip. Through the aromatic blend of his fair trade beans came a belated syrupy burn. I still had that SMS from yesterday on my phone from an unknown number. It had said simply:

IM OK HABIBI. X

'No, and I doubt I will again. She'll start again somewhere else, somewhere new.' I poured another shot into my coffee to give it a bit more of a punch.

'Just remember Spiderman, mate,' he said, watching me.

'I'd have to drink a hell of a lot more to catch up. Wish we could have stopped him.'

'He was gone a long time ago.'

'Still, somehow I think we failed, you know, as neighbours.'

'When I lived in Kreuzberg,' the Anarchist said, 'there was a story going round about a man living in one of the shittier communes. He was a drug addict who tried to eat himself. He carved little bits off his body and cooked them in the pan with lentils. He fucking tried to eat himself! I always wondered what the other commune dwellers were doing at the time when he was carving and cooking himself.'

'So much for the higher ideals of communal living.'

'Some of those who lived there were just drug addicts, opt-outs. Some had mental illnesses. Not all commune dwellers were there for idealistic reasons. It wasn't all sweetness and light, my friend. Remember that most moved into the vacated buildings a few years after the Wall came down. And not all for the same reasons. It was pretty run down and desperate in parts. Sometimes life was real shitty. Real tough.'

I remembered our brief visit to the *Kopi*, one of the last true squats left in Kreuzberg, and I remembered feeling a tad disappointed. In the grounds of the main squatted building festooned with bedraggled banners, was a junk-filled mini-maze of lean-to's, prefab dwellings and caravans, choked with collecting refuse, tarpaulin, spare car parts, shopping trolleys full of the spoils of scavenges and patrolled by quasi-feral dogs. An overgrown, unloved, neglected nirvana.

'And not all the politicised commune dwellers shared the same ideals,' he went on, putting his paper down, scratching his messy hair. 'In fact there were often disputes between the different communes on the same street. Sometimes over politics, sometimes over petty things.'

'You were struggling against the system. Why struggle against yourselves?'

'Human nature,' the Anarchist said. 'Struggle defines us all.'

'Maybe.'

'Only when things are tough, when we are faced with difficult situations, that we get to know our true selves. Recession, deprivation, persecution...'

'Wall partitions...'

'Wall partitions. They make men – and women – of us. Not indolence, not comfort. What have the Swiss given the world?'

'Euthanasia?'

'Hah! It is the struggle for utopia, not its attainment, that makes us what we are.'

The thorax was warming as the drink went down. 'You might be right, I said. 'Listen, I got news.'

'Will it be in the *Süddeutsche Zeitung*?'

'No. I have a job offer. In London. I have to go back.'

'Capitalism comes calling, eh? I expected you to go, to be honest. Will the police let you go?'

'On the condition I leave a contactable number and address. I'll give you another month's rent up front. Give you time to look for another flatmate.'

'Thanks. It's a shame. We had fun. You, probably too much.'

'But at least you'll get another try for a Scots flatmate.'

'True. Well,' he said, raising his coffee mug, 'end of a brief era. I would join you for an Irish, but I've got an interview this morning at another school… I know, I know, no religion or politics unless they ask.'

'Might be best to change your t-shirt for the interview, too.'

He looked down at his *Napalm Death European tour* t-shirt. 'Good point. What do I say if she comes around one day looking for you?'

I lowered my mug and looked at its tarry content. 'She won't.'

'I'll miss sharing our glass of whiskey,' he said.

'That and our debates about politics and philosophy, my friend.'

'You'll be back,' he said. 'And you never know, one day so might she.'

Lost weekend | Lyle

The display told him all he needed to know. But whether it was the residual effects of 48 hours' relentless intoxication, or the simple fact that he did not want to believe it, his mind took a while to register its import.

HEATHROW EZY7210 GATE CLOSED

Schipol's bright, modern airport buzzed around him: people with places to go, desks to check-in at, planes to catch. Not Lyle. His plane had gone, his seat unoccupied.

Head pulsing, nausea building, he checked his ticket for the umpteenth time, just in case the arrangement of letters had changed to reassure him he had made a mistake, that his flight was later, his flight...

Had gone.

Shit. Shit. Shit!

He wiped away the collecting sweat off his brow, caused by the desperate dash through the terminal, and pulled out his mobile phone. It was dead. He had run out of battery power and had not brought his charger. And now the boys would have theirs switched off and stowed away; no doubt finding his absence hilarious, rather than a concern. Mike would probably be grateful, as Lyle had not relayed to anyone yet the fact that he had found him thrashing about naked in a canal. For the others, Lyle's absence would be merely another amusing anecdote to add to the long list of humorous accounts of a their stag weekend. *Lyle had been so stoned he had missed his flight. Har fucking har!*

And then it struck him.

Whether it was the toxic legacy, the sudden realisation of what exactly he was rushing to get back home to, or whether it was more simply to forestall that expected ridicule, turn it on its head and write the end of that particular anecdote himself, Lyle decided to do an uncharacteristic and wholly unexpected thing. Rather than go to the airline's helpdesk, explain his dilemma and arrange another flight, he hauled his bag over his shoulder and headed for the airport's train terminus a floor below the airport's main terminal – to the platform that would take him back to Amsterdam.

14/11 | When the tide goes out

I had to have a whiskey this morning. Then a beer. I couldn't face the day straight knowing that she was not going to be a part of it. I sat on my balcony with the remains of a cold pilsner, Spiderman's typed papers on my lap, and soaked up Berlin's street scene for the final time. I looked at the four-storey cliff face of the apartment building opposite and, not for the first time, my mind made an unwelcome semiotic leap with the processed information. I looked at the rows of black-eyed windows with their quadrangles of glass panes and suddenly I saw a repeated pattern go down the street, and knew that that pattern would line almost every street in the district, if not the city. Countless numbers of white wooden cruciforms. Line after line, tier after tier, of crosses fixed into every apartment building façade.

Banishing the thought I toasted the slow dip of the sun. It made its way below the promontory of the tree-dotted hump of a hill on which squatted the remains of a wartime bunker. Up in the dimming dome of sky a crow had struck a thermal and was cruising in lazy spirals. 64 years ago a crow might have done the same thing in the same spot, returning to forage in a ravaged city. A desiccated rock shoreline exposed by the retreating tide. Head swivelling to fix a beady eye on the ground, what would it have seen through the toxic haze of countless unchecked fires? The revealed rock pools and coral reefs of gutted buildings. Craggy, jutting, ribbed, uneven and sharp. Dropping low now, sensing more spoils from man's ceaseless tussles, the crow headed for the pock-marked bunker crouched on the hill. That last vestige of Nazism holding out against the Soviet besiegers. Inside refugees – women, children, elderly men – sat huddled with young soldiers in ill-fitting uniforms. They were all looking up and flinching at every thud of mortar round and tank shell that chipped away against the massive carapace of the anti-aircraft battery, blinking and wincing at the falling dust and praying to indifferent Gods for it to stop.

Our history. Our past. It weighs heavily on us sometimes. It is a burden that does not lighten unless we are able to shift the weight, confront it, face it, learn from it and move on with it. It is a distant but insistent voice that says, 'Never forget me. Remember me and learn from what I have seen. Remember and move on.'

I downed the last of my beer. Time to move on.

Lightning Source UK Ltd.
Milton Keynes UK
17 April 2010

152972UK00001B/4/P